A snapping branch to the north snagged Weston's attention...

There was definitely at least one person in the forest. Kayleigh's eyes got wider. She'd heard it too.

A second rustling sound in the opposite direction alerted them to a second adversary.

Weston leaned close to Kayleigh's ear. He spoke in a low tone.

"Stay with me. Step where I do."

She nodded again.

Grabbing her hand, he moved quickly, aiming for spots of soft wood and moss to cover the sound of their steps. Behind him, Kayleigh did as he'd asked: stepped where he stepped, grabbed where he grabbed.

He knew she had to be scared—it was dark, there was thunder in the distance and people were chasing them. But she held it together.

And he was going to do whatever he had to in order to keep her safe...

TEXAS BODYGUARD: WESTON

USA TODAY Bestselling Author

JANIE CROUCH

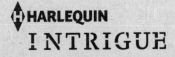

Since this book is about family, it's dedicated to my Kiddo #3.
You may not be a child of my womb, but you are very definitely
a child of my heart. You are brilliant, kind and extroverted to
the extreme. It is a great honor to be your mom.

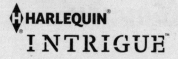

INTRIGUE™

Recycling programs
for this product may
not exist in your area.

ISBN-13: 978-1-335-59033-6

Texas Bodyguard: Weston

Copyright © 2023 by Janie Crouch

For questions and comments about the quality of this book,
please contact us at CustomerService@Harlequin.com.

Harlequin Enterprises ULC
22 Adelaide St. West, 41st Floor
Toronto, Ontario M5H 4E3, Canada
www.Harlequin.com

Printed in U.S.A.

Janie Crouch has loved to read romance her whole life. This *USA TODAY* bestselling author cut her teeth on Harlequin Romance novels as a preteen, then moved on to a passion for romantic suspense as an adult. Janie lives with her husband and four children overseas. She enjoys traveling, long-distance running, movie watching, knitting and adventure/obstacle racing. You can find out more about her at janiecrouch.com.

Books by Janie Crouch

Harlequin Intrigue

San Antonio Security

Texas Bodyguard: Luke
Texas Bodyguard: Brax
Texas Bodyguard: Weston

The Risk Series: A Bree and Tanner Thriller

Calculated Risk
Security Risk
Constant Risk
Risk Everything

Omega Sector: Under Siege

Daddy Defender
Protector's Instinct
Cease Fire

Visit the Author Profile page at Harlequin.com.

CAST OF CHARACTERS

Weston Patterson—One of the four boys adopted as a teenager by Clinton and Sheila Patterson. The most quiet and serious of them all. Owns San Antonio Security with his brothers.

Kayleigh Delacruz—Nature photographer and daughter of business tycoon Leo Delacruz. Childhood friend of Weston's.

Chance Patterson—Oldest of the Patterson brothers, and the most strategic. The caretaker.

Brax Patterson—The most charming and outgoing of the Patterson brothers. Married to Tessa, father to Walker.

Luke Patterson—Gruffest of the Patterson brothers. Willing to do whatever needs to be done to protect his family. Married to Claire.

Maci Ford—San Antonio Security office manager.

Sheila and Clinton Patterson—Adoptive parents of the four Patterson brothers.

Leo Delacruz—Billionaire business tycoon whose past is catching up to him.

Jasper Eeley—Leo Delacruz's head of security.

Gwendolyn Whitlock—Leo Delacruz's personal assistant.

Dean McClintock—Leo Delacruz's longtime attorney.

Prologue

"Weston?"

He heard a tap on his door and stiffened, backing away from the homework sitting on his desk. It was Sheila, the only female voice in the Patterson house.

He liked Sheila pretty okay. She laughed a lot. Got up every morning and made lunches for him and the three other boys who lived in the house.

She worked as a nurse every other weekend, only taking shifts when her husband, Clinton, would be home. Weston didn't understand that. It wasn't like he or the other guys needed a babysitter. He was thirteen. Clinton and Sheila's other kids were around that age too.

But Weston liked that there was always an adult around. And that the adults were pretty nice.

His dad hadn't been *pretty nice*. The opposite of pretty nice. Weston rubbed at a burn scar on his arm. One of dozens.

"Do you want me to come back later? That's no problem," Sheila said softly from the other side of the door.

That was another thing he liked about his foster mother. She didn't push.

"It's okay, you can come in." He had to force himself to use a loud enough voice for her to hear.

Weston was quiet. He'd always been quiet.

He'd been in multiple other foster homes before coming to live with the Pattersons three months ago. Most of the homes had been pretty good, but temporary.

He liked it here, even with three other boys—Chance, Luke and Brax—living in the same house. They were *not* quiet, but they didn't seem to mind if he was.

"School go okay today?" Sheila asked as she opened the door.

He nodded. Every time he'd gone to a different home, it had meant a different school. At least with this one he'd had someone to ride the bus with and sit with at lunch.

Brothers.

That's what they called each other. Brax and Luke had already been adopted by the Pattersons. They were in the process of adopting Chance.

Weston wasn't about to get his hopes up. Who would want to adopt *four* teenage boys?

But if they asked…

"I wanted to ask you something," Sheila said.

Weston's heart thumped in his chest. Was she about to ask him to be a permanent member of their family too?

He acquiesced with another slow dip of his head.

She continued, used to him not talking unless he had to. "I'm tired and don't want to cook, so we're going out to eat. I thought I'd ask you first if you had a preference for where we went. It's hard to get a word in edgewise with the other three."

Oh. Going out to eat, not asking him to be a part of the family. He was stupid to have even thought that might be the case.

Sheila took a step closer. "Hey, you okay? What just happened?"

He quickly looked down at the notebook on the desk. There was no way he was going to tell her what he'd been thinking.

"I like spaghetti," he said, barely loud enough for her to hear him.

It probably wasn't his favorite, but was the first thing he could think of. Hopefully it would keep Sheila from pushing to see if anything else was wrong.

It worked. "Okay, Italian it is. Luke will love you for it. I'll round everyone else up. Meet downstairs in ten minutes?"

He nodded. He didn't look up when she came closer. Didn't flinch as she slowly—making sure he was very aware of where her hand was— reached over and squeezed his shoulder gently.

Didn't say anything as she removed her hand a second later and left.

Ten minutes later, he headed down the stairs. He could hear the rest of the boys running around, bouncing a ball, yelling about some video game—the general chaos always present in the house.

As he waited, Weston silently stared at the photographs all over the wall. They were pretty chaotic—snapshots Sheila or Clinton had taken. Some of just the two of them, some with Luke, Brax or Chance in them.

A family.

No pictures of Weston, but that was okay. Sometimes there wasn't room for everyone.

But at least tonight he'd get to eat spaghetti.

Chapter One

Weston Patterson's eyebrows raised as his brother Brax ducked into his office and hid behind the door. "Do we have some sort of armed perp in the lobby I need to know about?"

Brax shook his head. "Worse."

It could only be one thing then. "Chance and Maci are at it again?"

"Yep. She erased his chicken scratches on the whiteboard and he's about to blow a gasket."

Maci Ford had been San Antonio Security's office manager for over a year now. The woman was a godsend when it came to organizing and running the office. Weston had no idea how they'd survived without her.

Two of his three brothers felt the same. Brax and Luke all but worshipped the ground her color-coded-file-categorizing feet walked on. Particularly because it meant they didn't have to do the filing themselves like they had the first five years their security and private protection business had been open.

But Weston's other brother, Chance, didn't quite seem to have the same appreciation for Maci. It was a source of constant entertainment for the rest of them to watch their normally unflappable brother get oh so flappable around Maci.

"Sometimes you can be a real jackass, Chance Patterson." Maci's words floated in from down the hallway.

Weston chuckled. "How long do you think it'll be before Chance threatens to fire her?"

"As soon as he does, you know she's just going to bring up her contract."

Maci couldn't be fired unless all four brothers agreed it needed to happen. And the way she'd helped them to get the office and business organized over the past year, nobody but Chance would even consider getting rid of her.

Not that Chance would. Weston loved to hear his brother get put in his place by the sassy office manager. Loved that she got Chance out of his own head.

Just like Weston loved seeing how relaxed Brax was now that he was married and had a son of his own. And how happy Luke was with his fiancée, Claire.

None of the four Patterson brothers were related by blood, but they were very definitely family. And there was no one else Weston would rather be in business with than these three men.

"Hey, Maci," Brax called out. "Do you think we can change our business cards to say Brax, Luke, Weston and Jackass Patterson?"

"I'll get right on it!" she yelled back without missing a beat in her mock argument with Chance.

Brax grinned, probably about to egg them on. Weston just shook his head. He'd always been the quietest of the Patterson brothers ever since they'd all been adopted by Sheila and Clinton as teenagers. He was never going to be as outgoing or friendly as his brothers.

Too many scars—both the ones marring his skin and the ones on his soul.

But that didn't mean he didn't enjoy being around them. His family accepted him for who he was. Didn't expect him to be chatty.

His cell phone rang and he grabbed it from his desk, frowning down at the info that lit the screen.

Leo Delacruz Industries.

That was not a call he was expecting; a huge blast from his past. He stared down at it as it continued to ring. Brax motioned to see if he should leave for privacy but Weston shook his head before answering.

"This is Weston Patterson."

"Weston, this is Leo Delacruz." The man's voice was still as authoritative as Weston remembered. "Do you remember me?"

"Yes, Mr. Delacruz, I remember." A bright summer in an otherwise dim time of his life.

"Good, good. I need to talk to you about your security services. Something important that I don't want to discuss over the phone. Can you come out to the estate?"

"Sure. I'll be glad to come out." Security for someone of Leo Delacruz's stature would be a boon for their business. "When were you thinking?"

"This afternoon at three. Unfortunately, danger doesn't wait for appointments or convenience. Do you remember the estate?"

"I sure do." It wasn't something Weston would ever forget.

"Good. I'll see you then." He hung up without another word.

Brax was staring at Weston, eyes almost comically wide. "Did Leo Delacruz just call you?"

Weston nodded. "He wants to possibly hire us."

Brax shooed that info away. "Leo Delacruz, the billionaire business mogul, just called you personally. Not through the office line, but on your cell phone. Knew you by name."

Weston rubbed his hand over his short-cropped

hair. "Yes. I worked at his house one summer as a kid, a few years before Mom and Dad adopted me. I was sort of an assistant gardener."

Not really. The truth was he'd been a nine-year-old kid who'd desperately needed wide-open spaces and his temporary foster father Henry—Leo's actual gardener—had realized that. Henry had brought Weston along to work with him and paid him a little out of his own salary.

"You knew Leo Delacruz in your past life and never once mentioned it." Brax shook his head. "Brother, you take the strong, silent type way too far. I would have that info tattooed on my forehead."

Weston smiled and rolled his eyes. "I was a kid. Haven't talked to him since. I'm surprised he remembers me at all."

He and Leo hadn't been close. But he and Leo's daughter, Kayleigh, had been nearly inseparable. He'd thought about her way too much over the years, even though neither of them had ever made any attempt to get in touch after that one summer.

"What are you going to do?" Brax asked.

Weston shrugged. "Show up at three."

And step back into the past.

THE DELACRUZ ESTATE had seemed like a castle to Weston as a boy, majestic and overwhelming.

The red-tiled roof had peeked out from over the tops of sprawling Mexican oaks, the beautiful arches and windows more amazing than anything he'd ever seen.

The property itself was on the outskirts of San Antonio, backing up to the Hill Country State Natural Area. Thousands of acres behind it that would never be built on made the Delacruz estate seem even more magnificent.

Now, as a grown man pulling onto a front courtyard large enough for a football game, the house didn't seem as overwhelming, but it was still impressive. Everything about it screamed money—the striking fountain at the center of the courtyard and the tan, brown and red stone comprising the exterior façade of the home that seemed to glow in the midafternoon sun.

Weston's eyes automatically landed on the grounds. Partially because of his love of plants and landscaping, which could be traced back to the summer he'd spent at this estate. But also to see the changes that had been made since he'd seen it last over twenty years ago.

It still looked amazing. The presence of flat, white landscaping stones that cut into the sloping ground running down from the front patio created a multilevel effect. Potted succulents and cheerful blackfoot daisies sat atop the stones, and they appeared carefully tended to.

Henry, Weston's first foster father, would've approved. He'd loved working here, loved explaining the plants and their characteristics to the timid Weston. Loved making the grounds at this estate as beautiful as they could be. But Henry had been gone a long time. Weston was glad to see Leo had not let Henry's hard work go untended over the years.

He parked and turned his attention to the enormous doors at the front of the house. He hadn't spent much time inside as a kid, not that he'd wanted to. Everything he'd wanted had been outside. The sun, a chance to move without having to worry about someone hurting him, and Kayleigh.

He rang the doorbell and a well-groomed woman in her midfifties answered. She gave him a warm smile. "You must be Weston Patterson. Mr. Delacruz is expecting you."

"Thank you." He stepped inside and she closed the door behind her.

Weston spotted two security guards immediately—one was using a tablet, undoubtedly to check Weston's appearance against his ID picture. The other was ready to make sure Weston didn't get any farther. That was a good sign. If all it took to get inside Leo Delacruz's house was to hack his calendar, his security team wasn't doing its job at all.

"I'm Gwendolyn Whitlock, Mr. Delacruz's assistant." She turned and walked quickly, efficiently, and he followed at her heels. "He's waiting in his study."

He remembered only some of the inside of the main house from his time here as a child. The gardener's shed was a different story—although how that two-story structure with running water, electricity and air-conditioning could be called a shed was beyond him. He'd loved that building. Loved when Kayleigh had snuck them Popsicles and they'd eaten them fast before they'd melted in the Texas heat.

Gwendolyn knocked on the study door and opened it. Leo Delacruz stood, smiling, then walked around the desk to shake Weston's hand. "Weston. Thank you for coming."

"Thank you for the invite." Weston shook his hand, marveling silently over how intimidating the billionaire had seemed when he'd been young. Then again, most everyone had seemed big and intimidating to an abused nine-year-old. "I'm a little surprised you remember me at all."

"Oh, I do."

Weston waited for him to elaborate, but he didn't. A broad-shouldered man stood a few paces from the desk, posture stiff, eyes taking in everything. Leo turned his attention that way. "This is Jasper Eeley, my head of security. Dean McClintock, my head counsel. And you met Gwendolyn."

The older woman and the lawyer inclined their heads with a small smile, but Jasper clearly had no intention of exchanging pleasantries.

Leo turned to his employees. "I need to speak with Mr. Patterson alone."

Gwendolyn immediately shook her head and informed Leo to let her know if they needed anything.

Jasper's posture stiffened further. "Do you think that's a good idea, Mr. Delacruz? I'd feel better if I stayed in here also."

The head of security looked to Dean to garner support for his argument. The lawyer nodded. "Jasper might be right."

Leo returned to his chair. "Mr. Patterson has been thoroughly vetted. I think I'm safe. If he kills me in cold blood, you two have my permission to have 'They told me not to do it' engraved on my tombstone."

Jasper didn't appreciate the joke. He left without another word, not concealing his glare at Weston as he went.

The lawyer gathered his papers and put them in his briefcase. "Are you sure, Leo? How you're handling this merger…it's not sitting well with me."

Weston didn't know what that meant, but he wasn't going to ask.

"I'm fine, Dean. This is all going to work out. Just wait and see."

Dean nodded and left with a great deal more grace than Jasper had.

Leo gestured to the seat across from his desk. "Is this place similar to what you remember when you visited as a child?"

Weston took the seat, studying Leo as he did so. His brown hair had gone gray over the years. But he seemed to be in decent shape, physically. Older, but fit. "I didn't spend a lot of time inside the big house, but yes, very similar. Still very impressive, Mr. Delacruz."

"Please call me Leo. I imagine you're wondering why you're here, exactly."

"It seems like you've already got decent security in place. I'm not sure what San Antonio Security can do for you that Jasper's team isn't already providing."

"I wasn't lying when I said you've been thoroughly vetted. Your agency comes highly recommended for personal security. I was looking for someone outside of Jasper's inner circle for a special assignment. When I saw your picture, I recognized you as Henry's kid. But your last name isn't Bogle."

"Henry was my temporary foster father, so I

never took his name. After he died, I was placed in another home."

Actually, a group home. And then another one. The foster care system sometimes wasn't particularly friendly to older kids.

Leo frowned slightly. "I suppose April didn't have it in her to continue fostering you after losing Henry."

"No. Losing him was hard for her. She decided to move to be closer to family. Because I was a foster child, I couldn't be taken out of the state."

"I tried to help her financially. But I had my own difficult time just after Henry's death."

Weston nodded. He honestly had no idea what had been going on with the adults during that time. All he'd known was that his life had changed immediately and irrevocably when Henry died. No more home. No more safe place. No more working here on the grounds with plants he was learning to love so much.

No more friend Kayleigh who liked to talk to him all the time.

"I'll get right to it then." Leo leaned back in his chair. "I've spent my life making money through mergers and business sales—decisions that destroyed companies and even some people's lives. I've made a lot of enemies in the past twenty years. That is why I have Jasper and his team around at all times."

"Understandable."

"I have a merger coming up in two weeks—it's actually two sets of separate mergers. I won't bore you with the details, but suffice it to say that there are people on every side who don't want these mergers to happen."

"And you think your life is in danger."

"I'm always in danger. It's a fact I've accepted."

Leo slid a file over to him.

Weston whistled through his teeth as he looked at the collection of threats received through multiple media—emails, pictures, spray-painted walls of one of the buildings he owned. Most of them told him to die, or that he would be killed, or would burn in hell.

"These are impressive." Weston raised an eyebrow. "I particularly like the one threatening to roast marshmallows over your burning corpse."

Leo could at least chuckle about it. "Doesn't seem very sanitary, does it?"

"Do you have leads on these?" Maybe tracking down where the threats were coming from was what Leo wanted from San Antonio Security. They could certainly work on it.

"Most of these are old. A few are current, but

we're aware of who sent them and have measures in place to prevent any marshmallow-roasting. More importantly, I've made it known that threats will not stop me from completing business. As a matter of fact, for any important mergers I make, there is a public clause in my will that stipulates my death will not stop the completion of the merger."

"Smart. Less reason to actually kill you."

"Exactly." Leo pushed another paper toward him. "What's worrying me is this particular threat that showed up two days ago via email."

It was one sentence printed over and over.

We know how to get to you.

No other threats, nothing dramatic. Just the statement.

"Are you upping security because of this? Is that why you want to hire us?"

Leo shook his head. "I am upping security, but I am concerned that the email may be referring to my daughter, Kayleigh."

Weston kept his face carefully neutral. "Kayleigh?"

"You remember her, right? She followed you and Henry around the entire summer."

Weston very definitely remembered. "I was glad to hang out with her. I wasn't used to someone wanting to talk to me as much as she did." He hadn't been used to having friends at all.

"You were special to her. She…" Leo trailed off. "Anyway, I am concerned that the threat in that email might involve her."

Weston sat straighter in his chair. "Maybe. Definitely shouldn't be discounted. But it could mean many other things too."

"Agreed. But until this particular merger is over, I want extra security on Kayleigh."

"It looks like you have plenty of security available to spare a team for her."

Leo leaned his elbows on his desk. "Kayleigh and I don't see eye to eye when it comes to her security. She refuses a live-in team. I don't like it, but she's made it clear if I want to be in her life at all, I'm going to have to accept it. I have a distant team on her, but that's not enough. Not with this new threat."

"What about this new threat makes you feel like it targets her particularly?"

Leo steepled his fingers. "Honestly? All of it. Someone saying they know how to get to me? The best way to do that—the only time someone has been successful in stopping any of my business mergers—was through hurting Kayleigh."

"Someone hurt Kayleigh?" Weston hadn't seen her since they were kids, but the thought sent a bolt of anger through him.

"It was a long time ago. One of my enemies

grabbed her to coerce me into doing his bidding. It worked temporarily, although I then made sure that person would never try anything like it again. But I won't take a chance on Kayleigh's life."

He was in wholehearted agreement. "How can San Antonio Security—" and by that Weston meant himself because if Kayleigh needed protection, he wanted to be the one providing it "—help?"

"Kayleigh doesn't like the restrictions having a bodyguard puts on her. She particularly doesn't get along well with Jasper or most of the men he assigns. She tends to give them the slip. I want you to be her bodyguard instead."

Weston wasn't surprised that she didn't want anything to do with Jasper given the man's less-than-sunny disposition. But still… "I can't guard someone who's running away from me. It's dangerous for both of us."

"She won't run. I'll talk to her." Leo checked his watch. "She should be awake and around soon, if she isn't already. Would you be willing to stay until I've spoken with her? Maybe walk around the grounds? Gwendolyn can provide anything you need."

Weston raised an eyebrow. Midafternoon and Kayleigh was just waking up? "Sure."

He could see if this place lived up to his memories.

Leo opened the double doors leading onto one of the covered patios, allowing Weston to step outside, then told him he'd send someone for him in a few minutes.

Weston walked the area, studying the landscaping that was just as ornate as when Henry had been in charge. There were a handful of colorful perennials clustered along the pathways leading around the wide, sparkling pool. Bougainvillea vines covered the patio roof, turning it into a purple cloud, while good old Texas wisteria grew farther off the beaten path, tucked into nooks closer to the house where they provided color and fragrance.

Also, the perfect place for an intruder to hide.

Hadn't he helped plant those bushes? Nine-year-old Weston obviously hadn't known much about home security.

He made a full circle of the home's exterior, eventually returning to the jacaranda tree at the southeast corner of the house, closest to the gardener's shed.

Their tree. His and Kayleigh's.

He rolled up his shirtsleeves against the sun's heat—though the shade made it cooler. Looking up, he caught patches of blue where the crisscrossing branches and foliage allowed brief glimpses of sky.

How many hot hours had he spent under this tree? Drinking lemonade, eating cookies Kayleigh had snuck out for them. Or the Popsicles that Henry had kept in his freezer.

The tree seemed to drip with memories... Kayleigh talking all the time and the way Weston loved to listen to her converse about everything. Dance class, television shows, the girl at school who kept buying the same clothes Kayleigh wore.

She'd been lonely. Looking back on it now as an adult, he could see it. But at the time, for a kid who'd found it so difficult to talk to anyone, being able to just listen had been a relief. He'd hoped Kayleigh would talk to him forever.

This tree held great memories. Even laughter. Not something nine-year-old Weston had done much of. Not something thirty-one-year-old Weston did much of either.

How many times had he wished that summer would never end? That the fascinating girl by his side would be his friend forever even though they were from different worlds?

He looked around now, taking in the expensive surroundings once more. Kayleigh was just waking up as his workday was almost finished.

A lot of things had changed in Weston's life since he'd known Kayleigh last, but they were definitely still from different worlds.

Chapter Two

Daddy, I'm scared. Please help me. I don't know what to do.

It was so dark but she didn't want to cry in case the bad man came back. How would Daddy know how to find her? Was she going to die just like Mommy?

She heard the footsteps. Oh no, it was the bad man. It was the bad man. He was coming back. He was...

Kayleigh sat straight up in bed, her back soaked with sweat, trying to claw her way out of the nightmare. Her eyes darted around the room. Where was she? This wasn't her house. Was she on assignment?

She caught sight of the elaborate floor-to-ceiling curtains. Everything clicked into place. No, she was at her father's house, in her old bedroom. Someone had pulled the blackening curtains too tightly. She would never normally keep herself in the dark like this.

The dark contained too many nightmares. Too many times the bad man tried to come back and get her. Even though she was no longer that ten-year-old and the bad man had died in prison years ago.

Kayleigh's breathing evened out and she sat up, swinging her legs off the side of the bed. She was jet-lagged, returning from a photography assignment in Indonesia, and hadn't been able to get to sleep until nearly dawn, so she still felt groggy—something she was used to with her profession as a nature photographer that sent her all over the world. It would pass. Even more quickly once she got to her own home and surroundings.

Her father had met her at the airport and brought her here, to his house, rather than take her to her own. She'd been too tired to fight again about not having live-in security and had reluctantly agreed to sleep in her old room.

Live-in security, especially one of her father's goons, was not an option. Her independence was the most important thing to her. If she wanted to have an unreasonable fear of the dark, that was her prerogative, as long as she could do it on her own.

Kayleigh got out of bed, pulling the curtains wide to let the midafternoon sun chase away the lingering darkness before getting dressed.

Thankful she rarely bothered with much in the way of hair or makeup, she made her way to the kitchen. She warmed up the plate of leftovers one of the housekeepers had left for her and sat down at the kitchen island to eat alone.

Nothing new about that. She'd been eating alone for years, even when she'd lived here. Her dad was always busy, and they rarely shared a meal.

Although it wasn't like she was really alone. There were security people all over this house, even in the far corner of the kitchen, although none of them talked to her.

She was halfway through her meal when her dad's assistant, Gwendolyn, came through the kitchen doorway. "There you are. I thought that jet lag might really take you out this time. How was Indonesia?"

Kayleigh smiled at the older woman. She was the most bearable of all Dad's employees.

"I liked it. It was a lot more rugged than I was used to. Perfect for the theme of the shoot."

"What was that again?" Gwendolyn snatched a bottle of water and came to sit next to her at the island.

"Surviving nature. Showcasing different plants that can kill humans and how dangerous they can be if they're not respected."

It had also been perfect to add to her secret

personal project about how certain plants survived even when they shouldn't. It was a passion project she'd been working on for years. Kayleigh hoped to someday make a book out of her collection of shots.

She spent a couple of minutes explaining her Indonesia shoot to Gwendolyn. She wasn't sure the older woman was truly interested, but she was at least pretending enough to make it seem so.

Indonesia had been amazing, even under the circumstances she'd been traveling, which definitely weren't luxurious—mostly camping in the wild. That was how Kayleigh preferred it. She would rather be alone with her camera and wildlife than in this giant mansion full of people, none of whom were actually listening or talking to one another.

"We're glad you're back, dear," Gwendolyn said. "Your father worries whenever you're not around."

Kayleigh somehow refrained from rolling her eyes. "Dad worries when I am around. The only time he doesn't worry is when I'm sitting right next to him."

Gwendolyn shook her head. "We can't blame him for that, can we, after everything that happened to you as a child?"

Given that Kayleigh was still having nightmares about it nearly twenty years later, blaming her father for still being overprotective felt hypocritical. "I guess not."

Gwendolyn had been working for Leo for three years now. She was a big improvement over the much younger assistants he'd tended to hire for the past couple decades, who may have been a pleasure for Dad's guards to look at, but weren't nearly as organized or as friendly as Gwendolyn. Kayleigh had hoped there might be some sort of romance between the older woman and her father, but that had never transpired.

Their conversation was interrupted by Jasper, Leo's head of security, storming into the kitchen straight to the coffee maker, pouring himself a cup without a word to either of them.

Jasper wasn't Kayleigh's favorite person on his good days. Jasper in a snit was completely unbearable.

"Everything all right?" Gwendolyn asked him. "You seem to be a little flustered." Part of her job was sometimes unruffling the feathers that Leo was quick to ruffle.

Jasper took a sip of his coffee then crossed his beefy arms over his chest. "Leo makes it a lot harder to do my job when he cuts me out of the loop."

The older woman raised an eyebrow. "I'm sure

he's not cutting you out of the loop on anything. You're his head of security."

"He is in there talking to some bigwig from a private security company. If he's got a problem with how security is being run here, he should let me know."

Kayleigh understood why her dad kept Jasper around. They both were very old-school, shoot-first-ask-questions-later type of men. Jasper reveled in asserting his power over others, and tended to hire men for his security team similar to himself.

Kayleigh concentrated on eating the rest of her food while Gwendolyn attempted to talk Jasper out of his pout—there was really no better word for his behavior. Kayleigh stayed out of it; she preferred talking to him as little as possible. At least now, after eating and shaking off the grip of the nightmare, she was feeling better.

"Ms. Delacruz, your father would like to see you if you have a moment."

Kayleigh was midway through one of her last bites as another member of the security team showed up in the doorway.

"Me too?" Jasper asked.

The man shook his head. "No, sir. Only Ms. Delacruz."

Kayleigh glanced over at Jasper, pretty sure she could see steam coming out of his ears. He followed behind her as she left the kitchen, despite not being directly invited.

She knocked on her father's office door. "Hi, Dad. You wanted to see me?" Jasper followed her inside but she didn't say anything about it.

"There you are, honey. How are you feeling?" Leo came from around his desk to give her a hug and she hugged him in return.

"A little jet-lagged, but otherwise not too bad."

She wasn't about to mention the nightmare and fear of the dark. That would lead to more arguments about security.

She pulled back, taking a seat. Leo sat in the chair next to her instead of going back around his desk.

"You should have just taken me straight home rather than bring me here from the airport, Dad."

Leo didn't even pretend to be repentant. "It was late, and you know how I already feel about you living in that house alone."

She swallowed a weary sigh. "We've been over this before."

"I know we have. But things have changed with my business. I'm dealing with some dangerous people and I would like for you to consider having live-in security until the merger is finished."

"Your business is always dangerous. That has

been true for as long as I can remember. So my answer is still no."

She'd learned over the years to make a firm stance from the beginning.

"Live-in security would be the best thing for you." Jasper took a step forward. "I'm willing to take on the assignment myself, if that will make you feel any more comfortable."

She knew her smile was completely false but there was nothing she could do about it. "No, thank you."

There was no way Jasper was going to be her live-in security. He and all the little clones he'd hired were part of the problem. But it was more than that.

She refused to give up her freedom, refused to have someone living in her shadow twenty-four hours a day. It would drive her crazy. Her privacy and independence were too hard-won and too important.

"You're just being stubborn," Jasper said.

Her fake smile slid away. "I'm not being stubborn. I'm a grown woman, and I have the right to live the way I want to."

"You know what? She's right," Leo said.

Both her and Jasper's heads spun around to look at him.

"What are you up to?" she asked. "You've

never given up a fight that easily in your entire life."

Leo let out a little chuckle. "Maybe I finally realize that arguing with you is pointless."

"Probably because I learned how to argue from you." She couldn't help but smile at her dad. He drove her crazy sometimes, and she knew his business practices were questionable at best, but she loved him.

Plus, his agreement with her made Jasper mad, so double bonus.

"How about if we compromise?" Leo said.

Her eyes narrowed. "Depends on your definition of 'compromise.'"

"You don't have any photography assignments for the next couple of weeks, right?" he asked.

"That's correct."

"What if I don't insist on any sort of live-in security—" Leo held out a hand to silence Jasper, who was obviously about to argue the opposite "—but you agree to stay in one of the family estates until this crazy merger I'm working on is over."

"Two weeks?"

He nodded. "Three at the most. After that, things should be much more settled."

Kayleigh studied her father through narrowed eyes. She'd learned over the years not to ask for details regarding his businesses. If he was really this concerned for her safety, then this merger must involve some truly questionable people.

"Fine. I'll stay at the Lake Austin house. Will that work?"

"Yes, that will work well," Leo concurred.

Jasper immediately excused himself. "I need to go check on a few things around the house, sir, if that's okay?"

"Yes, go ahead." Her father shooed him with his hand.

As soon as Jasper closed the door behind him, she turned back to Leo. "You know what he's doing, right? He's going to set up security at the Lake Austin house right now. I'm sure he'll come back in a couple of hours with some elaborate plan to present to you."

Leo let out a little chuckle. "Subtle, Jasper is not. And I also know you're not going to Lake Austin, so why don't we talk about what your real plans are?"

Kayleigh couldn't help but smile. "I hate the Lake Austin house. You know that. I'm going to Lake Ray Roberts."

She expected more of an argument from him, but he actually looked pretty pleased at her announcement.

"I thought you might say that." Leo slipped an arm around her. "I promise I won't let Jasper know. But, fair warning, I've already scheduled some landscaping work to be done out at Ray Roberts. So don't freak out if you're not alone."

She shot him a side look. "Is the landscaper one of Jasper's men?"

Leo squeezed her shoulder. "Definitely not. I promise."

"Fine. As long as I don't have anyone following me around in a suit and earpiece, then I'm good. I'll head out in the morning."

He kissed her on the top of the head. "Thank you for humoring your old man. I'm hoping this merger is the last one that might potentially bring danger to our doorstep. It's…different than some of my others."

The phone on his desk rang, so she gave him a little wave as he answered and she left his office. Rather than go back to her room, she turned to the left, deciding to walk outside.

She knew why she did it. She'd long since stopped trying to deceive herself about why she walked outside whenever she was at her dad's house. She wanted to go by the jacaranda tree. Their tree. Hers and Weston's.

Except for its purple blooms in the spring, the jacaranda was pretty unassuming. Not as big as many of the other trees or colorful as the other plants. Nobody tended to pay much attention to it.

But today someone was under the jacaranda,

tending to some of the shrubbery around it. She wasn't familiar with any of Dad's current landscapers and wasn't going to say anything. But as she walked by, the man stared at her from where he was crouched.

"Be careful with that tree. It's important to me," she said.

"I'm glad to hear that, Kayleigh."

Something inside her mind shifted at the sound of the voice. She could now see traces of the little boy she'd known in the features of the man in front of her. Her eyes grew big.

"Weston? Is that really you?"

She blinked rapidly in surprise, taking in his dark skin and handsome face, his strong jaw and close-trimmed hair. She couldn't believe he was really there. He wasn't dressed like a gardener. He was in dress pants and a white shirt with a tie that had been loosened and sleeves rolled up, yet his hands were covered in dirt from whatever tending he'd been doing.

Putting on makeup or fixing her hair hadn't seemed important after the nightmare, but now she wished she'd taken the time.

He saw her looking at his hands and gave a sheepish shrug. "Sorry, I was here for a type of interview with Leo. When I saw this tree, I couldn't help but get in here and make things a little more perfect."

This was exactly how she remembered him, always handling plants, reverent for the nature around him. But he definitely wasn't that nine-year-old boy anymore. The Weston in front of her was a man, strikingly handsome, with intense brown eyes.

"I'm tempted to do the same every time I walk by this tree," she said. "Not that there's anything wrong with it. Dad keeps this place landscaped to within an inch of its life. But sometimes I just like to get my hands dirty."

He brushed the soil from his hands off to his side. "I understand you're a nature photographer, so I guess you get your hands dirty regularly."

"Yeah, I love it." Had he kept up with her over the years? The thought gave her a weird thrill in her chest.

"Then it sounds like a wonderful profession."

"Are you going to be doing some work for Dad?" Weston was obviously still in the landscaping business.

"Yes, actually," he said. "I—"

"Excuse me. Mr. Delacruz wants to talk to you now, Patterson." Jasper walked up and interrupted them. "You shouldn't be out here talking to Ms. Delacruz anyway. That's not your place."

She shook her head. "Calm down, Jasper. Weston and I know each other from when we were younger." Although his name hadn't been Patterson then.

Jasper crossed his arms over his chest. "It doesn't matter. He shouldn't be talking to you."

She turned back to Weston. "Don't listen to him. It's fine."

Weston shook the rest of the dirt off his hands. "No, Jasper's right. I should get back to Leo if he's waiting for me. But it was good to see you."

"Yeah, it was good to see you." They gave each other small waves, Jasper making it all awkward, and Weston left.

Kayleigh turned back to look at the jacaranda and the work Weston had been doing underneath it. He definitely wasn't the silent little boy she'd followed around that summer after her mom died.

Maybe staying here at Dad's house wouldn't be so bad if it meant she could run into Weston each day while he did gardening work.

But no, she couldn't. She'd fought too long and hard for her independence. Staying here would be a step backward. She wouldn't do that.

Not even for the brown eyes that had enthralled her just as much today as they had back when she was a kid.

Chapter Three

Weston remained quiet following Jasper back to Leo's office. Silence, a survival mechanism as a child, continued to work in his favor as an adult. Many people took his reticence as a sign of weakness.

Their mistake.

"Thanks for waiting," Leo said as they arrived back in the office. "I talked to Kayleigh and she has agreed to live-in security until this merger is complete."

The older man turned to Jasper. "Can you prep a security detail for the Lake Austin house? You know the property best."

Jasper barely hid his preen. "I'm already on it." He glanced over at Weston. "If it's okay with you, sir, I think we should not use any outside team members for this situation."

Leo nodded. "You have carte blanche. Do whatever you feel is necessary to make sure that property is secure."

Weston didn't say anything as Jasper left the room with a smirk. He wasn't offended by Jasper not wanting him on the team. Their style would not blend well.

And if Jasper was who Kayleigh had agreed to, then it was not Weston's concern. He certainly had no business being disappointed.

Just like he'd had no business getting so caught up talking to her outside—in studying the details of her face, the soft huskiness of her voice, tamping down the urge to touch a strand of her long brown hair falling out of her loose braid.

"This is the Lake Austin house I was referring to." Leo passed an electronic notebook across the desk.

Weston thumbed through the images. "It's impressive." The damned thing was hardly anything less than a mansion.

"It's got two separate guardhouses and security rivaling a military base. I wish that's where Kayleigh would go to stay for us to keep her safe."

Weston slid the tablet back across the desk, raising an eyebrow. "It's not?"

Leo tapped something on the tablet then slid it back to him again. "No, this is the Lake Ray Roberts property. This is where she's going."

This house was much smaller and, to Weston's

eyes, much more appealing. He looked through the photos of the grounds. They were much more natural, less landscaped.

"You approve of that house more than the big one."

Weston shrugged. "Let's just say it's more my style than anything quite as ornate as your Lake Austin property."

"Kayleigh basically feels the same way. She wouldn't last two days at Lake Austin with Jasper's men before they drove her crazy and she took off." He pointed at the tablet. "But she's agreed to stay here, and you can guard her if that works for you."

"Yes." Weston kept his answer simple, although he was feeling a lot more. Hell yes, he wanted to make sure he was the one keeping Kayleigh safe, especially somewhere like this. If she'd agreed to it, he was all in.

"The property doesn't have a lot of amenities, but it's got plants for days." Leo pointed at a slight bit of dirt that had gotten on Weston's shirt. "It looks like you still have an affinity for plants, like when you were a boy and came with Henry."

Weston brushed the spot. "I do. I spend a lot of my free time in the dirt."

Leo seemed pleased with the news. "The Ray Roberts property is completely off the radar, which is why I'm not bringing Jasper in on this. If you can keep it casual, Kayleigh is much more likely to feel comfortable around you. Not running from her own security detail is going to keep her much safer."

"Agreed."

"If you want to do some gardening work while you're there, I'm happy to pay you a little extra. Kayleigh loves plants too. That's why she became a nature photographer. She'll probably relax more around them."

"No need to pay me to work with the plants. I'm sure I won't be able to stop myself from messing with them anyway."

Leo conceded with a slight dip of his head. "The property has a separate gardener's unit right next to the house—has running water and electricity. Does that suit you? I don't want to put Kayleigh in a situation where she has to stay in a house with someone she doesn't know."

"That's fine. I'll set up security for the main house so I know if anyone is around other than the two of us."

Leo gave him a smile. "Good. Bill me for whatever you need to purchase. Kayleigh is planning to arrive tomorrow afternoon."

"Then I'll head there tonight and make sure security is the way I want it to be."

"Spare no expense. Whatever you need. Kayleigh's safety is the most important thing." Leo pulled out a file containing keys, maps and entry info, and handed it over.

Weston turned to leave but then stopped. "Leo, are you sure you don't want to go with Jasper? He may not be her favorite person, but he seems diligent when it comes to security. Changing things up might be a mistake."

Leo stared at him for a long minute before turning to look out the window. "Mistakes. I've made a lot of mistakes with Kayleigh. Made a lot of mistakes all the way around."

"Like what?"

"When Kayleigh was—" The man shook his head, cutting himself off. "Things happened to Kayleigh not long after you knew her before. I won't go into details, but I have smothered her too much over the years to make up for it. But not in the way I should have. I constantly threw more security at her when I should've been taking more time with her myself."

"It's not too late to make that change."

"That's what I'm hoping. That's why these last two mergers I'm working on are so important. It will help right some of my wrongs over the years."

"Can you tell me more about the mergers? Maybe we should be working this from both ends—protective detail but also figuring out how to stop potential danger before it starts."

"Everything centers around Brighton Pharmaceuticals."

Weston had heard of the company but didn't know much more than that. "Big name."

Leo rubbed the back of his neck. "I'm ruffling a lot of feathers on damned near everybody with this transaction. I have my team looking into the threats."

San Antonio Security would be looking into it also. A fresh set of eyes never hurt. And Weston wanted to know everything he could going into this situation.

"I'm willing to take the job, but I want to make sure this is really what you want."

"What I want doesn't really matter. What matters is keeping Kayleigh safe. Fixing things." Leo scrubbed a hand down his face, looking older than he had a few minutes ago. "Kayleigh struggles. She doesn't like to have people in her personal space. I'm hoping that will be different with you. You were special to her."

She'd been special to him too. "It was a long time ago."

He looked back out the window. "She asked for you, you know, after Henry died. Didn't understand why you couldn't come back. I should've made more effort to find you. Especially after…"

He trailed off again then straightened in his chair. "Let's just say that keeping Kayleigh safe is the most important thing in the world to me. The two of you in a location no one else knows about is the best way to make that happen."

"I will keep her safe, I promise."

Weston didn't make promises lightly.

"That's what I was hoping you'd say." Leo stood up. "Now go get whatever you need to keep my girl safe. And don't forget to work on the plants too. That's what will help her feel most at ease."

WESTON WASN'T SURE, exactly, what it said about his life that he could take off for an undetermined amount of time and it barely be noticeable.

If it wasn't for his parents and brothers, he had no idea how introverted he would've become. From the day he'd met Clinton and Sheila Patterson, they had slowly and gently eased him out of his shell. His talkative brothers had done the same.

But outside of his family, Weston was very much reserved and liked to be alone. Even during his three years in the San Antonio Police Department, he'd had a reputation for being a loner.

So the only call he'd had to make to slip out of his regular life for two weeks to allow him to protect Kayleigh was to the office. Nobody else would even realize he was gone.

It was getting dark as he dropped by his apartment to grab some clothes and his personal weapons. His Glock 19 was rarely away from his body, but this situation also called for some other firearms.

While packing, he made a call to Chance. Since his other brothers had families now, he didn't want to bother them. Chance was single, like Weston, and he would be the best at digging up intel on the potential threats surrounding Brighton Pharmaceuticals.

"Hey," Chance answered after the second ring. "Heard you're besties with Leo Delacruz."

Weston shrugged and put a couple of T-shirts in his duffel bag. "I see Brax hasn't lost his flair for the melodramatic. But yeah, Delacruz wants to hire us for a security detail."

"Okay. Do I need to get it on the schedule?"

"No, I'm going to do this one myself. Live-in security for two to three weeks."

There was a moment of silence from Chance. "So you are Delacruz's bestie."

"I knew his daughter back when we were kids. She doesn't like the current security team, so Leo wanted to see if she'll do better with me."

"Fair enough. At his estate?"

"No, we're going to a property at Lake Ray Roberts. I'll send you the info."

"You're not usually one to volunteer for live-in security. Cuts into your alone time."

He added some socks to the bag. "I guess I'm willing to do this one for old times' sake."

And because, if anyone was going to protect Kayleigh, Weston wanted to be that person. Even though they came from opposite worlds and probably had nothing in common.

Maybe he was doing it for kid Weston, who never had the chance to get closure with that friendship. Or maybe for the Kayleigh who had been such a good friend then and needed help now.

Or, if he was honest, probably because he'd never been able to get her out of his mind as a kid, teenager or adult.

"I need you to look into this merger Delacruz has, involving Brighton Pharmaceuticals. See who has the most to lose by it."

"Has he gotten direct threats?"

"Mostly vague, but I'd like to know what we're dealing with. Maybe you can get intel Delacruz can't because they're watching for him to make a move."

"Smart. We'll get on it."

He finished putting the rest of his clothes in the bag. "And can you ask Maci to clear my schedule for the next couple of weeks? I don't have much on the calendar, but some of it will need to be juggled."

There was a long moment of silence from Chance. "Why are you asking me to do that?"

"Because I'm on the phone with you, dumbass. When you see her tomorrow, ask her for me."

"Right. When I see her tomorrow."

What in the world was going on with his brother? "Are you okay, Chance? Had some sort of head injury in the last few hours I don't know about?"

Chance was the most sharply focused of all his brothers. This behavior wasn't like him at all. Then Weston heard a woman's voice in the background at Chance's house.

That explained it. Or at least some of it. Chance dated quite a bit, but he'd never known any of the women to be a distraction.

"Never mind, you have company. Didn't mean to interrupt."

"It's no problem. I'll be sure to give Maci the message. Tomorrow. When I see her."

Whoever Chance's guest was had him pretty tied up in knots, judging by his stilted sentences. Weston chuckled. "Thanks, bro."

He disconnected the call, finished packing and headed out the door.

A few hours later, he was pulling up at the Lake Ray Roberts property.

He'd already gotten what he'd needed at the defense and tactical gear store on the outskirts of San Antonio. His contact had been willing to open up for him despite it being after business hours. Some of it was out of respect for their security firm, but mostly it was because Weston was able to flash Leo's cash at him.

He looked around as best he could in the dark. Using this remote property, rather than one of the more elaborate homes Leo owned, was a good tactical plan. But Weston still wanted electronic backups in place in case they were necessary.

He let himself into the house with the key Leo had given him and walked through it. There was nothing too special about it—two bedrooms, one set up as an office. Living room, eat-in kitchen. Front of the house had the most windows since that faced the lake. The gardener's unit was a bedroom and bath. No view of the lake, but very close to the house—perfect for security needs.

He was up at dawn the next morning and drove as far as he could around the property, then got out of his car and walked around it to familiarize himself. It was everything it had looked like in the pictures—wild and lush. Definitely not the manicured elegance of the Lake Austin mansion Leo had shown him. Weston would take this house any day of the week, not just because it was better for security, but because of the nature surrounding them.

As far as Weston was concerned, lawns needed to become a thing of the past. They'd been a show of wealth and status in the seventeenth century. No need for them anymore. Give him indigenous trees and plants any day.

But right now he didn't care about the plant life around him, except for how it affected security.

He spent the entire morning setting up sensors he'd bought that would let him know if there was anyone else on the property besides him and Kayleigh. He put sensors near the road and along anything that even remotely resembled a path leading toward them. He placed even more sensors around the house, and in all the windows and the doors, keeping them as unobtrusive as possible.

Hopefully, keeping them out of sight would help Kayleigh to relax with the security. He wanted to do that for her, not just because it would make his job of protecting her easier, but because he wanted her to be relaxed. He wasn't sure what it was Leo had been alluding to that had happened to her, but it hadn't sounded good.

He walked down to the water. The lake itself made security more difficult. They'd be able to hear an engine, but anyone using stealth would be harder to monitor. He set up sensors along the shore, but made mental note of this potential hole.

Once he had the property the way he wanted, he got back in his car to familiarize himself with the wider area surrounding them. There was a marina a couple miles away by car, so he decided to rent a boat, using Leo's money, and had it delivered. That could be used as a backup getaway vehicle if they needed it.

He also stocked up on groceries and, since they had a decent gardening section at one of the stores, went ahead and bought some of the things he would need to work the land. He had some ideas of what he'd like to do landscaping-wise. It would enhance the natural beauty of the area.

By midafternoon, he was confident about the level of security he'd set up. Secrecy would still be their best defense, but the devices he'd put into play would notify him if there was trouble.

Now all he had to do was wait for Kayleigh to arrive. He changed into some more suitable clothes for gardening and decided to go ahead and tackle some of the landscaping until she got there. The monitor systems he'd set up would let him know when she was nearby. The system was a good one. He was confident in his own experience and ability to keep her safe.

He was much more prepared for whatever danger may come than he probably was for the woman herself.

Chapter Four

From the moment Kayleigh left her father's house the next morning, she was craning her neck to check her rearview mirror, expecting to find Jasper or one of his men tailing her. Dad had said Jasper wouldn't be around, but she wasn't sure she could trust that.

The temptation to just go to her own house was strong. The thought of being followed around, never having any privacy, someone standing outside her door while she was sleeping…she couldn't do it. Even for a few weeks. Tension pooled through her whole body at the thought.

That was one of the reasons she took so many photography jobs out of the country. There was still security involved, but never somebody assigned only to *her*, watching every move she made. Nobody who asked why she slept with a light on or sometimes had nightmares. Nobody to pry into her secrets.

The way she wanted it.

She was still a little jet-lagged. The shoot in Indonesia had been brutal on her body. Lots of waiting and holding still for long hours in difficult weather—including storms, which were never her favorite. She'd had to force herself to work through them despite the mental anguish they caused.

So she hoped Dad would keep his word and keep the security team at bay while she had her R and R. Might as well be at the tiny lake house nobody liked but her.

The farther she drove with no cars following, the more she relaxed. This close to the relatively barren section of Lake Ray Roberts, it would be impossible not to see a tail. Dad had kept his word.

She let out a little curse when she arrived at the cabin and saw another vehicle parked by the house. Damn it, Dad *hadn't* kept his word. She gripped the steering wheel until her knuckles were white.

She was about to leave when she saw someone working over in the overgrown shrubbery, and relaxed a little. It wasn't a guard; it was the gardener Dad had mentioned. He or she wouldn't pay much attention to Kayleigh at all.

Then the gardener stood and twisted in the afternoon sun. A thrill shot through her.

Weston.

She'd been a little sad when they hadn't been

able to talk more before she'd left the main house, but definitely hadn't expected to see him out there. As a matter of fact, now that she knew his last name—Patterson—she'd been considering calling him to see if he wanted to get together for coffee sometime.

Now she didn't have to.

Weston straightened as soon as he saw her and walked toward the car. She gave him a little wave and smiled as she got out. "I didn't expect to see you here."

He shook his head. "You mean Leo didn't tell you I took the job?"

"No. He told me that someone would be here, but didn't mention it would be you."

A few awkward seconds passed between them before he tilted his dark head to the side. "Is it okay with you that I'm here? Leo and I agreed this would be where I would be most effective. He thought I could stay at the gardener's house, out of your way. But you have to be okay with it all."

"Yes, absolutely." Her smile became bigger. "I'm glad to see you. Believe me, my dad wanted me to go somewhere else, but that would've involved Jasper and his security goons following me around every second."

He stood straighter and crossed his arms over his chest. "Ms. Delacruz." His brows furrowed and voice became way...too serious. "I think having at least a dozen men assigned to your every step would be the best sort of security anyone could provide."

His imitation of Jasper was spot-on and she laughed. "Weston Patterson, did you just make a joke?"

"I guess I did. Although, in my defense, Jasper is an easy target." He gave her a smile that showed a tiny dimple at the corner of his mouth. "Can I help you bring your stuff in?"

"No, I don't want to interrupt what you were doing. I can carry it in myself."

"It's no trouble. I'm just messing right now. Trying to come up with an overall plan. This place is a dream in terms of flora."

She nodded. "Yeah. I love it here—the wild, natural beauty of it all."

He took out her suitcase, and she grabbed the camera equipment she never went anywhere without and brought it into the house. Immediately she could see the kitchen had been well stocked.

"I wasn't sure exactly what you liked," Weston said. "So I got a little bit of everything. Leo paid for it, of course."

She was a little surprised her father had told Weston she was coming at all. Probably had warned him to stay away from her. Dad could make things so awkward.

She turned to him, putting her camera down

on the kitchen counter. "Listen, are *you* okay with me being here? I know we haven't seen each other in, like, twenty years, so if it's not okay, please let me know."

He gave her an odd look. "I would have never taken the job if I wasn't okay with being around you."

She was making the situation even more awkward. Better to just leave it alone. "Great! Then would you mind terribly if I change clothes and come out to help with some of the gardening and landscaping?"

He smiled, that dimple coming out again. She found herself staring at it. "Absolutely. Leo gave me carte blanche to change and put in whatever I saw fit. That was a mistake."

She laughed out loud, tearing her eyes away from his mouth. "Oh yeah, it was. Let's show him how much."

All the tension she'd been carrying was gone. Dad hadn't gone behind her back and sent a guard. Instead, she'd have a long-lost friend to spend some time with.

A *sexy* long-lost friend.

She couldn't think of anything better.

"This isn't your job, you know," Weston said, looking over at Kayleigh, who was covered in dirt.

Again.

Nearly every minute for the past three days he'd been working with plants, she'd been out here with him, doing whatever needed to be done.

Not just the gardening stuff most people liked to do—putting seedlings in the ground or decorative trimming. She'd done the nonglamorous stuff too—carried and spread fertilizer, weeded, pruned larger trees and bushes—all over the property. Never once did she decide to go hang out at the dock or stay inside and watch TV.

Weston was convinced Leo Delacruz was flatout incorrect when it came to judging his daughter. She'd been nothing but polite and wonderful to be around. She hadn't tried to run off once, hadn't told Weston to back out of her personal space. She'd been…normal. Helpful.

And sexy as hell in the dirt.

He'd told Leo as much—minus the sexy as hell part—every day when he'd reported in via phone call. Leo had been happy to hear it, since the threats against him had been escalating.

So far, there had been no sign of trouble here. Weston almost felt bad for how much Leo was paying him, since all he was really doing was working with the land and enjoying Kayleigh's company.

"I know it's not my job, but I love digging around in the dirt." She beamed up at him from where she was kneeling in the soil. "And I do

a lot more of it than you think as a nature photographer."

He knew all about her career. Had for years.
Probably more than was healthy, and definitely
more than he planned to share with her. "I'm
glad you found something you love to do."

She looked back down at the blue flag iris she
was planting. "I'm pretty sure my career can be
traced back to that summer with you and Mr.
Henry. It's where my love for plants started, although the photography came later."

"For me too. I'll always be thankful for the
time I had with Henry. Definitely started my
love affair with plants."

She let out a sigh, touching the bright purple
flowers in front of her. "I think I like plants more
than people sometimes. They can be so resilient
even while some look so fragile."

He couldn't stop his smile. "I'd choose hands
in the dirt than hanging out with people any
day."

They both worked in silence for a few minutes.

"I like being outside. Sometimes being inside
is…"

He waited for her to finish, but she didn't. He
twisted to look at her around the shrub he was
trimming. "Being inside is what?"

Her sigh was soft and a little heartbreaking. "Being inside is hard for me."

"How so?"

She paused for so long, he didn't think she was going to answer. She waited until she'd put the roots of the iris in the dirt and began covering them up before finally responding. "Being inside…sometimes I feel like I can't breathe."

"Like claustrophobia?"

"Yeah, but not exactly. Something happened when I was younger and…" She looked away. "I don't really want to talk about it."

He left the shrub and walked over to her, pulling off his glove. He touched the smooth skin of her arm. "You don't have to talk about it. I understand not wanting to talk about the past, believe me. Although I'm here if you want to."

She squeezed his hand. "Thank you."

"Tell me about Indonesia then. That was your last photography assignment, right?"

She gave him a relieved smile and they both got back to work. For the next few hours, she talked about Asia, then another trip she'd made recently to Iceland, and some others in America. He knew about a lot of them, but wasn't going to tell her that—what would she think if she could see the scrapbook he'd made of the photoshoots she'd done? He'd tracked her career for years from afar, never dreaming she would remember him at all.

She was talking about her Iceland trip and nature's resilience as evidenced by the plants she was shooting, growing in hardened lava, when she stopped suddenly.

"What?" he asked. Her insights had been intriguing, her passion obvious. Nothing about what she'd been saying had suggested it was difficult for her to talk about. "Is this hard to talk about too?"

She let out a wry laugh. "No, not at all. I stopped because this can't be interesting for you. I've been talking nonstop for hours. Aren't you bored?"

"Absolutely not. You were talking about tillandsia and its remarkable ability to grow under the harshest of circumstances. How can that not be interesting?"

Of course, he was pretty sure she could read the phone book and it would be interesting.

She shook her head, sitting back in the dirt, grabbing a sip of water from the bottle. "It's just like when we were kids. I'm doing all the talking. You can't get a word in edgewise. It must be frustrating."

The opposite. Her voice, her words, were soothing to him. "I like to listen. I've always liked to listen more than talk." Especially to her.

"Are you sure?"

"Believe me, yes." He'd be willing to listen to her voice all day every day. It eased something in him. Always had.

But he did his best to try to talk more the rest of the afternoon. Asked questions, interjected comments and even told a few brief stories of his own. He was about to call it quits for the day, so they could go put together dinner like they had for the past three nights, when a sudden storm blew up on them.

The rain covered like a blanket, soaking them within just a few seconds. Laughing, Weston grabbed their tools, and they ran for the gardener's cabin. Thunder shuddered in the air around them and the evening sky turned much darker.

"I am soaked!" He lined up the tools in their proper place as he shook his head, flinging water everywhere. "That was better than a shower."

His smile faded as he turned toward Kayleigh. She definitely wasn't laughing. She was pale, her arms wrapped around her middle, blinking rapidly at the sound of the rain beating on the overhang above them.

He cupped her shoulder as gently as he could. "Hey, are you okay? Did you get hurt?"

Another bolt of thunder. A huge flinch from her. "No. I...no." But her voice was barely more than a whisper.

He cupped her other shoulder, rubbing his fingers over her tense muscles gently. "How can I help?"

"You can't. I'm fine. I…" She pulled back and he dropped his hands. "I'm fine. But you know, I don't think I'm up for dinner. I'm going to make a sandwich and go on to bed."

"Kayleigh…"

Thunder crashed and she jerked, tendons standing out on her neck. "I have to go. I'll see you tomorrow." Without another word, she dashed the short distance over to her cabin and went inside.

Weston didn't know exactly what had just happened, but he knew for sure things were not all right.

Chapter Five

Weston sat straight up in bed, sleep gone in an instant. Something was wrong. He immediately reached for his weapon on the nightstand next to him.

Waking up this way—with a knowledge something wasn't right—was a habit his brain had developed as a child. It had saved him more than once when his abusive dad had been coming for him, allowing Weston to escape and hide. It had helped him in other foster care situations when bigger kids had decided to sneak up on him when he was sleeping.

It had taken almost a year after living with the Pattersons' constant affection and patience before that defense mechanism had learned to stand down.

But now it was back.

He moved out of bed in his gym shorts, slipping on the shoes lined up at the side of the bed, but not stopping to put on a shirt. He headed out the door and toward the main house, staying in the shadows, eyes searching for anything that was amiss.

The storm had burned itself out hours ago. None of the sensors had gone off to alert him of an intruder, and a quick search of the property also resulted in nothing. But Weston knew something wasn't right—his instincts were still going wild.

The door to Kayleigh's cabin was locked, so he used his key and began searching the front rooms first. No sign of forced entry.

Then he heard Kayleigh cry out from her bedroom.

He bolted back to her room, weapon raised, ready to defend her from an attacker. But there was no attacker. There was only Kayleigh, thrashing in her bed in the dimness of the night.

It only took a second to realize she was caught in the grips of a nightmare. A bad one.

Realizing there was no immediate threat, he lowered his weapon and slowly approached the bed so not to suddenly startle her. She cried out again as he knelt by her side, placing his gun on the floor before speaking to her in a soft, soothing voice.

"Kayleigh, can you wake up for me, sweetheart?"

"No. Please don't hurt me. Please. Please. It's too dark."

Her voice was odd. Not at all the way it normally sounded. It was higher pitched, softer.

"Daddy will come for me. I won't die like Mommy." She wrapped her arms around herself and rocked back and forth. "Please come get me, Daddy."

Weston's spine straightened. This wasn't a nightmare at all. This was a *memory*.

She had kicked off the sheet with her thrashing around, so he reached out and laid a gentle hand on her bare arm. "Kayleigh, you're safe. It's okay to open your eyes."

"No! I'll be good. Please don't put me back in the dark."

He looked over at the bathroom. The light had gone out. He'd noticed she'd kept it on at night, but tonight it was dark. He rushed out to turn on the switch in the hallway to at least give her some light when she woke.

"No, I'll be good. Don't hurt me. Please. Please. I want my daddy."

The sound of her voice, so small and frightened, caused his heart to clench. He knelt by the bed again, gently sliding a wisp of her brown hair off her face.

"Kayleigh, it's Weston. You're safe. Can you open your eyes? You're safe, sweetheart."

He kept murmuring soft words to her, easing her hands away from the bedsheets as she balled them up and started to scratch them down her arms.

"No dark. No dark. No dark."

"It's not dark here, Kayleigh. Open your eyes, you'll see."

She finally did. She sat up, sobbing, arms held out in front of her as if to ward off a blow.

Weston eased himself back. He knew what it was like to need a second to figure out what was going on, for the mind to adapt back to reality.

"It's Weston," he whispered. "You're safe. It's okay."

She turned and stared at him with her big green eyes. He wanted to touch her again, but wasn't sure if that might make things worse. He'd never wanted to be touched coming out of a terror-filled sleep. She might not want—

She launched herself into his arms, sobbing.

He caught her automatically and lowered them both to the floor so she was sitting across his lap.

Then he just held her. Let her cry out all her pain. Hated to hell that she had so much pain to cry out. He'd had no idea.

He held her until the sobs subsided and the shaking stopped. She all but drooped across his chest, but that didn't bother him a bit. He kept his arms wrapped around her.

"I'm sorry," she finally said with a soft hiccup. "I still have nightmares sometimes. It was the storm that triggered it."

"Something bad happened to you." It wasn't a question.

She nodded, still curled up in his lap. "Yes, but it was a long time ago. I... I was kidnapped."

"What?" He'd had no idea, and he knew a lot more about her life than either she or Leo realized.

"Dad made sure it was kept out of the press." She took a shuddery breath, her voice still shaky. "Someone was trying to use me to force Dad to change a business decision. He didn't want to give anyone else ideas."

If Leo was here, Weston would lay into him. Not letting Weston know about a previous successful kidnapping attempt, no matter how long ago it had been, made Weston less effective at protecting Kayleigh.

But Leo wasn't here. Kayleigh was, and she needed his attention.

"I'm so sorry that happened to you." His words felt so inadequate.

She shrugged one shoulder. "As far as kidnappings go, it wasn't so bad."

"I doubt that."

"Comparatively, it really wasn't." He ran his hand in gentle circles on her back, more than glad she was still cuddled up against him. "I was taken from school, smacked around a little, kept in a dark closet."

"That's why you like a light on at night. The one in the bathroom went out, so I turned on the hall lamp."

"Thank you. Believe it or not, I would've been more of a wreck if I'd woken up and it was completely dark."

He pulled her tighter against him. "How long did they have you?"

"Three and a half days. It was dark almost the whole time." She let out a little sigh. "The only thing I could hear was a storm, although I found out later that was a noisemaker they'd put on the other side of the door."

"Not surprising a storm triggered you then."

She shook her head. "It's been twenty years. You would think I'd be over it by now, especially with all the therapy I've had. And a lot of times I'm okay, but sometimes…"

"Sometimes the triggers catch you off guard," he finished for her. "They're vicious bullies."

He knew that firsthand.

"Yes, exactly."

He tucked a strand of hair behind her ear. "I have some triggers of my own, so I understand. And age or time away from the trauma sometimes doesn't matter at all."

"It happened just a few weeks after the summer you were working at the house. That was a really hard time for me. Mom had died the year before, then one day you stopped showing up. I didn't really understand what had happened. Even when Dad explained Henry had died, I thought you could still come. I thought you didn't want to be my friend anymore."

"Oh God, no, Kayleigh." He pulled her closer. "If there had been any way I could've gotten back to see you, just to say goodbye, I would've done it. My life got turned upside down after Henry died."

"I know," she said quickly. "I understand that now, of course. As a kid, I didn't have much frame of reference. I didn't even really understand that Henry wasn't your biological father."

"I wish I could've been there for you. I'm so sorry."

She leaned back so they could see each other eye to eye. "We were both caught up in situations we couldn't control. I wish it had been different for both of us. You were my best friend, even if it was only for the summer."

He leaned his forehead against hers. "You were the only friend I'd ever had. Those weeks I spent with you and Henry are some of the best childhood memories I have. But I wish I could've been there when you needed me."

He would've found a way. If he had known, even at ten years old, he would've found a way to get back and help her through it.

She cupped his cheek with her hand. "I was okay eventually, although Dad was completely overprotective for years—still is. And like I said, comparatively, it truly wasn't that bad. Some bruises and scrapes. A lingering fear of the dark and storms."

He'd seen enough in his line of work, as both a police officer and with San Antonio Security, to recognize her words as truth. It truly could've been much worse. But that didn't mean she hadn't suffered.

"It was more than what most people go through in their whole lives, so don't discount the trauma."

Her hand fell back into her lap. "I feel like a baby."

"You don't let it control you. That's what's important. Not that you don't get scared, but you set it aside when you need to. You haven't locked yourself away in a tower with twenty Jasper clones, as I'm sure Leo would like."

"Yeah, Dad would be thrilled if I agreed to that." She gave him a watery smile. "Thank you."

He smiled. "Do you think you can go back to sleep?"

"I don't think sleep is in the cards for me tonight."

"It's nearly dawn. How about if I make us some coffee and breakfast, and then we go out on the boat today?"

Her smile got bigger, some of the twinkle back in her green eyes. "That sounds absolutely wonderful. Thank you."

He hated to let go of her so she could get off his lap, but was glad she was feeling stronger. They got up and he kept a hand at the small of her back as they headed into the kitchen.

He hadn't been there for her when young Kayleigh had needed him, but he could be here for her now.

"How's it going, bro? Ready to pull your hair out yet?"

Weston was getting the boat ready to take Kayleigh out on the lake when Chance called.

"Would you believe me if I said I'm actually enjoying myself?" And it was true, except for the part of Kayleigh's nightmares terrifying her.

"You mean the great, silent loner is enjoying spending multiple days with someone? Inconceivable."

Weston rolled his eyes at his brother's impression of a famous movie line even though Chance couldn't see him. "You find out anything on Leo Delacruz's merger?"

"Brighton Pharmaceuticals is the company he's buying out, and it's not friendly. Owner is a Beau Kesler."

Chance sounded much more like himself than when Weston had talked to him a couple of days ago. That was good. He needed Chance focused.

"Never heard of him. Any arrests or history of violence?" Weston asked.

"Nothing that we can find," Chance replied. "He stands to make money from the merger even if it's a hostile takeover."

"Who stands to make the most from the merger not going through?"

Following the money was almost always a good place to start an investigation.

"We're looking into it. There are a number of competitors that will be hurting if the merger goes through. We're concentrating on a guy named Oliver Lyle right now. He's already got some red flags."

"What kind?"

"The violent kind," Chance said. "No arrests, but ties to the type of people who I wouldn't want to run into in a back alley without my side-arm."

That wasn't what Weston wanted to hear.

"Okay. I know Leo has his own team, and I

don't want to step on their toes." Although, admittedly, irritating Jasper would be pretty fun. "Find what details you can so I can be ready if they decide to come calling. Right now, keeping Kayleigh hidden is probably our best bet."

"Agreed and will do. I'll touch base soon."

Weston loaded the rest of the food for today's boat picnic. Hopefully, it would get Kayleigh's mind off the nightmare. "Thanks, Chance."

"Anything for my favorite brother."

Weston chuckled. They all called each other their favorite when the others weren't around. It had been a running joke for years.

"Just one question though," Chance said.

"What's that?"

"Is your client pretty? Do you have a crush on her? Is she the future Mrs. Weston Patterson?"

Weston told Chance in no uncertain terms what he could do with himself.

His brother was still laughing when Weston hung up the call.

Chapter Six

Kayleigh had been dealing with her nightmares alone for as long as she could remember. Her dad had tried to help when she was a child and then, knowing he was out of his league, had sent her to a therapist.

And while that had helped, the nightmares had never quite gone away.

As an adult, she'd hid them from everyone, especially her father. Nightmares would give him one more reason to smother her with security.

But it was often hard to handle the aftermath of her night terrors alone. It took hours, or sometimes even days, for her to feel back to normal.

Yet here she was a few hours later, her body and mind having rebounded almost like the episode—and it had been a bad one—had never happened. She knew why.

Weston.

She should've been embarrassed that he'd seen her at her most weak, but wasn't. Everything he'd done had been damned near perfect. He hadn't smothered her, had just offered his support—physically and emotionally.

And now they were trolling the bass boat he'd rented around on the lake, enjoying the sunshine. She took a bite of the sandwich in her hand, trying not to be affected by the sight of a shirtless Weston in low-slung jeans at the front end of the boat.

She was affected.

She finished her sandwich and snapped a picture of a sandpiper as it flew across the calm waters, very well aware that she'd also caught Weston in the shot. She'd *somehow* managed to catch him in most of her shots today.

"That's not your normal MO." He looked over his shoulder at her.

She grimaced at his words, sure she was busted for taking his picture.

"It's not?"

"That's not your normal camera, right?"

Thank goodness, he wasn't calling her out on being a pervy perv, shooting him without his shirt on.

"Yeah." Her voice came out as a squeak so she started again. "Yeah, this is my film camera rather than digital. Despite my squeamishness in the dark last night, I really enjoy developing film in an old-fashioned darkroom. It's therapeutic."

"A darkroom isn't totally in the dark, right?"

"Only for a few seconds when you're first taking the film out of the cassette and putting it in the tank. But I know that darkness is coming and I control everything about it, so it doesn't frighten me. The rest is done with a red light that doesn't harm the film."

"Sounds unique."

She smiled. "I enjoy working with the prints. It's almost a lost art. Shooting with a film camera is different than digital too. It requires me to be more precise and deliberate in my choices."

He stretched his long legs out in front of him and took a bite of his sandwich. "Did you study photography formally or were you self-taught?"

She shrugged. "Both, I guess. I did major in photography in college. I minored in horticulture. A blend of both my loves."

"I minored in horticulture also. Majored in sociology."

"You went to college?" As soon as the words came out of her mouth, she wanted to take them back. How obnoxious of her. "I just mean in your line of work, I didn't think a college degree was necessary."

He didn't seem to be offended, thank goodness. "I guess it depends on what aspect of my line of work you're referring to."

She agreed. "Right. You have your own business, so college makes sense. But sociology? That's an unusual choice." She didn't want to stick her foot in her mouth further by including the rest of the sentence...*for a landscaper.*

He looked out at the lake and then back to her. "I wanted to understand the system and figure out how to help kids who were trapped in it like I was. I'm not sure what form that will eventually take, I just know it will happen. I was a cop for two years, but figured out quickly that wasn't what I wanted to do full-time, so I went into business with my brothers. It keeps me pretty busy."

She had so many questions. His brothers were in the landscaping business too? He'd been a police officer?

But mostly, *"Brothers?"*

He grinned. That dimple was back and it was all she could do not to grab her camera and take a close-up of his face.

"I was bounced around the foster care system from the time you knew me with Henry until I was adopted by the Pattersons when I was thirteen. They adopted three other boys around the same age."

"Wow. Here I was thinking you were an only child like me. I guess if you guys went into business together, you're pretty close."

He pulled his phone out of his pocket and stepped over to her to show her a picture.

"This is Luke." He pointed to a white man. "He's the oldest by a few months. And this is Brax." That man was biracial. "He's married now and has a son."

He pointed to the Hispanic man with his arm around Weston in the photo. "And this is Chance. He's probably most similar to me—a little more quiet than Luke or Brax."

All four of them were completely different in skin tone and looks, but each so handsome. And obviously very comfortable with each other. *Brothers.*

She grinned at him. "Wow. You guys are like quadruplets. How do people tell the Patterson brothers apart?"

Weston belly laughed as he sat back down— the deep boom of it echoing across the water. It was possibly the most wonderful sound she'd ever heard.

She grabbed her camera, taking multiple shots, uncaring about whether it wasted film. She didn't stop even when his laughter died out. He was studying her, eyes serious, completely unselfconscious about the lens pointed at him.

He wasn't looking at the camera at all. He was looking at her using the camera. She finally set it down.

"I like to watch you work," he said.

"I like to hear you talk about your family and see you laugh. Will you tell me more?" She walked to the front of the boat so she could sit closer to him.

"Sheila and Clint Patterson—Mom and Dad to me and my brothers—are definitely unique. There aren't many people who would adopt four traumatized adolescent boys. I'm sure it wasn't always easy for them. They didn't have much money or space in their house. But they were patient and consistent with their love and acceptance, and eventually…" He shrugged, trailing off.

"Eventually they became Mom and Dad," she finished for him.

"Yes, exactly. If there's one thing I've learned, it's that family isn't always blood, and blood isn't always family." He touched a small circular scar on his shoulder as he said it.

She'd noticed similar ones on his back and chest too, and had wondered what they were, but hadn't wanted to ask.

He saw her looking at them. "Cigarette burns." His voice was stoic.

It took her a second to process that, then horror set in. "From your biological parents?"

"My mom died when I was five. My dad—my biological father, he was never a *dad*—wasn't thrilled about being saddled with a young kid. He drank. He was a mean drunk."

She reached for his hand, grateful when he didn't pull away. She knew that talking in general was hard for him. Talking about this had to be nearly impossible. But just like he'd been there for her this morning, she wanted him to know she was here for him now in whatever way he would let her be.

"The first time he burned me was on my ninth birthday. But, ultimately, those marks were what caught the attention of social services and got me out of there, so I'm kind of glad it happened. And eventually got me into the greatest family ever, albeit via a long and twisted road."

She wanted to wrap her arms around him, but settled for holding his hands. "I'm glad you have a family. That you have wonderful parents and a set of identical brothers." She nudged him with her shoulder.

He brought their entwined hands up to his lips and kissed the back of her palm. "Thank you."

"And I have to admit I'm a little jealous. I always wanted a big family. Obviously, by the way I monopolize every conversation, I needed someone to talk to."

His brown eyes met hers. "How about if I take you to meet my giant talkative family sometime? You won't be able to get a word in edgewise."

"I'd like that."

And with that, he seemed to be all talked out. They finished their sandwiches and cranked the speed up on the boat a little more. She took him to the north side of the lake to another house her father owned, one more similar to the ornate mansion at Lake Austin.

As they pulled closer, Weston slowed the boat down. The house and grounds, so grandiose and impressive, sat empty, like it did almost year-round.

Plenty of money, plenty of room...no family. A pretty close metaphor for her life. She had her dad, but their relationship was often strained. She had money, but was still often alone.

She didn't want Weston to see her poor-little-rich-girl attitude, so she pulled out her camera and started taking random pictures of the house. She was hardly concentrating on it at all, just allowing her mind and body to do what was almost muscle memory. She took shots of the grounds, the windows, the roof.

Nothing that she really wanted photographs of.

"Hey." Weston's hand touching hers on the camera finally had her dropping it. She was out of film anyway. No more hiding.

"Hey." She tried to sound chipper but failed miserably.

"You're sad." Those deep brown eyes met and held hers. She couldn't look away.

"What I am is ridiculous. Feeling sorry for myself when right in front of us is proof of my family's riches."

"We both know money is not what makes someone rich. And it's okay to be sad when you know you need something but you don't have it. It's like your abduction—just because it wasn't the worst that could've happened doesn't mean it wasn't bad."

"You know, for someone who doesn't talk very much, you sure have a way with words."

He smiled. Gah, that *dimple*. "Oh yeah? Well, why don't you let me make you a special dinner tonight and then you can really be impressed?"

The words set butterflies a'flight in her stomach. When was the last time she'd had someone cook a special meal for her because they'd wanted to? When was the last time she'd *wanted* someone to?

She was still feeling those same butterflies a few hours later when they made it back to their side of the lake, docked the boat and went inside. After a shower, she wished she had something better to wear than jeans and a T-shirt. Something more feminine and a little sexy.

She hadn't been prepared for Weston when she'd packed for this trip.

Night had fallen and he was already at work in the kitchen, having showered and changed himself. She was a little sad he'd donned a shirt, but loved the look of the ice-blue color against his brown skin. And was all but drooling at the way the muscles of his arms stretched against the tee's sleeves.

His arms had felt so strong wrapped around her this morning. Like he was powerful enough to fight off any demon that would dare try to haunt her.

"Okay." He turned to her, somehow aware of her presence in the doorway even though she hadn't said anything. "This meal won't be quite as impressive as I'd hoped due to lack of ingredients. But I make a mean salad to go with spaghetti."

She walked over and hopped up to sit on the counter next to the stove. "I'm a sucker for a good salad. Especially if it has exotic ingredients in it like tomatoes."

He pointed at her with the spoon he'd been using to stir the sauce and winked. "You just wait until we're not stuck here anymore. I'll make you a proper meal with ingredients much more exotic than tomatoes."

She couldn't help it. She reached out, gripped the front of his shirt and pulled him to her.

His lips were the perfect combination of soft

and firm—everything she wanted them to be. She wanted to pull him even closer. To lose herself in the kiss.

But then he pulled back.

It stung. Tension floated in the air between them. His eyes were so serious as they pinned hers.

She let out a nervous laugh. "Sorry. Don't know what I was—"

She didn't finish her sentence. He reached over to turn off the stove top.

Then his lips were back on hers.

One hand slid into her hair, the other wrapped around the small of her back and slid her closer to him on the counter. He tilted her head so he had better access to her mouth, and when she gave a surprised little gasp, he took advantage of it, teasing her tongue with his.

She draped her arms around his neck, pulling him closer. She shuddered as he deepened the kiss, senses reeling as his tongue demanded more of hers. She slid even more forward until their bodies pressed up against each other. Both of them moaned.

And then the power blew, leaving them in darkness.

Chapter Seven

The sudden darkness didn't throw her into a panic. She was too busy attempting to recover from that kiss. "Wow, I've never had a kiss so explosive it blew the power."

She expected Weston to make his own joke, but he had frozen and was looking down at his phone. "We've got trouble. We need to get out of the house."

She stared at him. Maybe he *was* making a joke and she just wasn't getting it. But the way he slid her off the counter and dragged her to the other side of the kitchen did not seem like much of a joke.

He opened a lower drawer and pulled out a gun.

"How did that get there?" she asked. And, even more importantly, why had he known it was there?

He put a finger over her lips. "Quiet. They're coming in through the back."

She stared at him with wide eyes. "What? Who's coming through the back? What are you talking about? How do you know?"

How could he possibly know?

"I set up perimeter sensors on my first day, just in case." He pulled out his phone and showed her where they'd been tripped, coming in from the west side of the property.

She blinked at him in the dimness, still trying to wrap her head around what was going on. "How would you know to do that? Did my father tell you to do it?"

He pulled her into the living room to the corner by the small couch, putting a hand on her head to keep her low. "It's my job and I take it seriously." His voice was more gruff than normal. "Your dad said you're skittish about security, so I didn't tell you about the sensors. Let's discuss this after we're out of danger."

They heard a creak toward the back of the house. She let out a little gasp. "So what do we do now? Should we run?"

Weston looked at his phone again. "There seems to be two of them. I need to take them down while they're not expecting it."

Take them down? Everything about him screamed warrior—his tone, his stance, his focus.

The opposite of the friendly gardener she'd been working with all week.

"You know how to do that?" she whispered.

"Your father would've never hired me as protective detail if I didn't." He pressed the gun into her hand. "Safety is off, if anyone comes in here who's not me, shoot."

He was gone before she could respond.

She blinked against the darkness.

Protective detail. Not the friendly gardener at all. He'd tricked her. Her stomach roiled in anger and pain. He'd lied to her, using their past to make her compliant.

The sickening sound of flesh hitting flesh followed by a moan dragged her out of her own head. She jerked, swallowing a little sob, as a gun went off not far outside the house.

Her head spun in that direction. Oh God, was Weston okay? She had no idea what he was like as a bodyguard. Either way, no matter how angry she was, she didn't want him hurt.

What should she do? Should she try to help him? What if he'd just been shot?

The darkness was pressing in on her, much more frightening now that she was alone. She couldn't afford to let the fear swallow her. She pushed away from the corner where Weston had stashed her and started moving along the wall. She needed to get outside and see if she could help.

She made it into the kitchen, barely able to

hear anything over the sound of her own jagged breathing, when a hand wrapped around her mouth from behind. Terror pooled in her gut.

But a moment later she heard a whisper in her ear.

"It's me."

Weston.

She sagged in his arms. He released her mouth and she spun to look at him. "Are you okay? I heard a gun."

"There are two unsubs out there."

"Unsubs?" She didn't even know what language he was speaking.

"Unknown subjects. Bad guys. I wounded one of them and they both took off. But we have to get out of here, they will bring back reinforcements."

"How do you know?" she asked, handing him back the gun he'd given her.

"It's what I would do."

It was what he would do.

She didn't really know him at all, did she?

"Let's go," he said.

"Hang on. Let me grab my camera. It's right here on the counter."

She wasn't leaving without it. She wrapped the strap of her camera bag across one shoulder and grabbed her film camera and purse too. She didn't know if they'd get any of her other belongings here back, so she was bringing as much as she could with her.

They were out the door a few seconds later. He led her away from where her car was parked. She wanted to ask exactly where they were going, but he motioned for her to keep quiet. They moved silently through the bushes near the edge of the lake then ended up on a side road where he had a car hidden under some shrubbery.

"You are certainly prepared," she said.

He gave her a one-shouldered shrug. "It's my job to be prepared."

"Wasn't there anything in your cabin that you wanted to get?"

He shook his head as they got into the car. "No, there was nothing in there I wasn't prepared to walk away from in an instant. I try to be that way for any job."

Any job. This had all been a job for him.

He began driving without the headlights on and she sat in the passenger seat, arms wrapped around her middle. Everything she thought she'd known for the past few days was coming unraveled. The Weston she'd enjoyed so much spending time with didn't actually exist.

He reached over and she thought, for just a second, he might be trying to comfort her. She needed it. She didn't understand and she was upset, but she needed his touch.

Instead his hand slid past her as he reached into the glove compartment and pulled out some sort of satellite phone. She recognized it from when she did shoots where the team was totally remote. The phones were expensive and could make calls from anywhere in the world, cell signal or not.

She knew who he was calling before he even started talking.

"Leo, we've just had a kidnapping attempt on Kayleigh."

She could hear her father yelling, although she couldn't make out the exact words.

"She's secure. We're headed back to San Antonio." Another pause. "They didn't expect that I had set up sensors, so I caught them unaware. I wounded one, but there was at least one more. I'm sure they'll be coming back with reinforcements, so we got out. We'll regroup at your house and figure out a plan from there."

Her dad said something else and then Weston disconnected the call.

"Are you okay?" He glanced at her briefly before looking back at the road. She wasn't sure how he could see, driving without his headlights on, but he was doing a remarkable job.

Was she okay? She didn't even bother to answer. He didn't seem to notice her lack of response. He just kept looking to make sure they weren't being followed.

It wasn't until they were out on the highway that he finally turned on the lights and seemed to relax a bit.

"We're all right. If they weren't following us by now, there's no way they'll find us on the highway."

She wasn't sure what to say to that, so she didn't say anything.

"Hey, are you okay?" Now he reached over and grabbed her hand. "You don't need to be afraid. We're safe now."

She looked down at his big, strong, capable hand holding hers and slid her hand away from him. She was too conflicted to touch him right now.

"I'm not afraid." That at least was true. "I'm mad."

"Why?"

Why? She shook her head. "You know, I expected lies from my father. He's never made it a secret that he will tell me all sorts of lies as long as it justifies protecting me. But I expected something different from you. I don't know why. I don't really know you at all."

"When have I ever lied to you?"

"You told me you were the gardener."

"I never said that." His thick brows were furrowed. "I told you I worked for your father, but I never said that I was the gardener."

"I thought you were the groundskeeper, like Henry. Obviously, you're much more than that."

He was quiet for a long minute. "I thought you knew. I truly did. San Antonio Security, the company I formed with my brothers, specializes in personal protection. Leo contacted and hired me because he thought you might be more comfortable if you had a guard who you had a kinship with."

"And all the plant stuff?" she asked.

He shook his head slowly. "I wasn't trying to fool you. Leo told me I was welcome to do any landscaping. That's what I love to do, and I thought you liked doing it with me."

She stared out the window for a couple of miles. She *had* liked doing it with him. She had enjoyed spending time with him more than anything else she could remember in years, but she couldn't help but feel betrayed. One more person who had tricked her. She'd opened herself up to him not really knowing who or what he was.

The rest of the drive back to San Antonio was made in silence. At some point, two more cars met up and flanked them. She knew immediately that was Leo sending out reinforcements when she saw Jasper driving one. Sure enough, the satellite phone rang.

She couldn't hear what was being said, but it didn't take much to guess.

"No, Jasper, she's fine where she is. She doesn't need to get into your car. We'll see you at the house." Weston hung up, cutting Jasper off midsentence.

His words made her more angry. "I see you're making decisions for me just like Dad. Nice." She knew she was being childish, but she couldn't help it.

He looked over at her calmly. "Would you prefer to ride with Jasper? We can stop and you can get into his vehicle. It's probably armor fortified, so it would actually be safer."

"No, I don't want to ride with Jasper, but it should be my choice."

He only nodded, which made her even more upset. But the problem was she wasn't really angry. She was *hurt*. That was worse.

As soon as they pulled up in front of her father's house, she was out of the car. She removed her camera equipment and looked back at Weston.

"Your services are no longer needed. I'll make sure Dad pays you for the time you spent with me."

She slammed the door and walked away.

Chapter Eight

Weston sat at his desk, watching the sunrise through the windows of San Antonio Security, thinking about Kayleigh. Thinking about her face when she'd realized he was her bodyguard—how hurt she'd been.

So when she'd gotten out of his car, he hadn't gone after her. He'd understood her need for space.

Instead, he'd followed Jasper—his smugness almost tangible after seeing Kayleigh storm into the house—to Leo's office and debriefed them both on the attempted kidnapping. He'd remained cool and professional. Jasper would be taking over and sending some men out to the lake to see if anything could be found.

After reporting, Weston had left. He wasn't needed as protection detail at the house, Leo hadn't asked him to stay, and Kayleigh definitely didn't want him around anymore.

He gripped his coffee cup tighter. He may

have remained quiet and professional while talking to Leo, but it had taken effort to push down the fury that had pooled up inside him.

Kayleigh wasn't the only one Leo had tricked. The man had put his daughter's safety on the line by not giving Weston all the information needed to protect her. He'd ruined whatever trust Weston had managed to build with her. She was convinced that Weston had lied, and hadn't even stuck around to try to find out the truth.

Not even after that earth-shattering kiss. She'd decided he wasn't worth her time anymore. Whatever had been growing between them had been lost.

Before he could think better of it, he smashed his hand into the filing cabinet.

"Whoa, there. What'd that cabinet ever do to you?"

Weston turned to find Chance lounging against the door frame. Clenching his jaw, Weston didn't even bother to check his hand. He already knew nothing was broken, just a slight ache across the side.

"What are you doing here so early?" It was barely past dawn.

"I could ask the same of you." Chance tilted his head, eyes roving over Weston's wrinkled clothes. "Aren't you supposed to be with—"

"Assignment's over," Weston said shortly.

He didn't want to discuss Leo's lies. Or the way Kayleigh's lips felt against his. Or the look on her face when they'd parted ways. He squashed the temptation to hit the filing cabinet again.

"What are you really doing here? We don't open for another hour."

Chance shifted his shoulders. "Trying to get some work done before Maci gets in and starts pestering me. Wasn't expecting to have to referee a fight between you and the filing cabinet."

When Weston didn't answer, Chance stepped farther into the room, folding his arms over his chest. "Seriously, Wes, what's wrong?"

Weston scrubbed a hand down his face. It was in his nature to be silent, but his family had never let that stop them from getting him to open up. "Kidnapping attempt on Kayleigh."

"Unsuccessful, I assume."

"Yeah, I got her out, and everything is fine. But there was a…misunderstanding between her and I. Doesn't sit well with me."

Because even now he was wondering if she was okay. It had been a hard night for her.

Chance's head cocked to the side. "You knew her before the assignment. You care about her."

He narrowed his eyes at his brother. Chance saw too damned much. "Yeah, we knew each other for a summer when we were kids, before

Clinton and Sheila, but we hadn't seen each other in years. She's a photographer now."

And yes, he did care about her. More after spending the last few days so closely with her.

Chance's eyes got wide. "It's *that* Kayleigh. You've been collecting her work for years."

Weston winced. He'd made the mistake of leaving the scrapbook he'd created of Kayleigh's photographs out one day when his brothers were over and they'd seen it. No point denying now. "Yeah, the same."

"And something happened between the two of you that has you beating up the poor, defense-less filing cabinet? Does she blame you for the kidnapping attempt?"

Weston explained how Leo had played them both and that Kayleigh felt betrayed. Weston couldn't blame her.

"Ouch." Chance blew out a breath. "You need to talk to her."

He sighed, rubbing the sore spot on the side of his hand. "She doesn't want to see me and I'm not going to force her to."

"She's only refusing to speak to you because she thinks you lied to her."

"It's not just that..." Weston trailed off, un-sure how to voice what he was thinking. Chance waited him out. He was family. He was used to Weston needing a little more time to be able to get his thoughts out vocally. "I'm worried about her."

Ultimately, it was that simple. He was worried about her safety. What if she decided to run from her security detail and made herself an easy target?

But mostly he was worried about her emotional health—she was fighting demons no one was aware of and he didn't want her to have to go through that alone anymore.

"Explain it to her, Wes. Tell her the truth."

"What if she still doesn't want me as her bodyguard?" Weston asked. "She doesn't like her father's men and, after this, she's not going to let anyone close enough to actually keep her safe."

"Look, you can either go and explain things to her or you can walk away."

Chance shrugged when Weston glared at him. He wasn't walking away from Kayleigh. Not again. He'd only had her back in his life for a few days and he already didn't want to know what it would look like without her.

Chance grinned. "That's what I thought. Which means your only option is to make her believe you. Tell her the truth, Wes. She'll listen."

Weston let out a long breath. Chance was right and they both knew it. He walked over to his brother and clapped him on the shoulder. "Thanks, man."

"Anytime."

Before anything else could be said, the front door chimed and Maci walked in. Both her and Chance's slight smiles immediately dropped into scowls when they saw each other, forcing Weston to choke back a laugh.

"Good morning, Maci," Weston said.

"Good morning, Weston. Oh, look, Chance is here too." She sounded anything but enthused at the sight of her least favorite Patterson brother. "I must have done something terrible in a past life to deserve Chance Patterson before I've had my morning coffee."

"You and me both," Chance muttered.

Weston wondered who would punch him first if he suggested the two of them get a room. Neither of them seemed ready or able to admit their attraction to each other even though it was definitely there on both sides.

They were still bickering with each other when he walked out the office door. Regardless of Chance's inability to realize his own feelings about Maci, he was right about Weston's.

Weston needed to talk to Kayleigh.

"I NEED TO talk to you." Kayleigh stormed into her father's office after Weston left.

At Leo's side, Jasper tensed at her entrance, reaching for his gun and only relaxing when he realized it was her. She didn't care if her fury was making his job a little harder. He'd already tried to talk to her twice since she'd gotten back with Weston a few hours ago, wanting to know exactly what had happened from her perspective.

"Get out, Jasper," she snapped, not taking her eyes off her father.

Jasper stiffened and turned to Leo. "Sir—"

"Give us a minute," Leo said.

Jasper scoffed under his breath and stormed out, shutting the door with something close to a slam.

Kayleigh couldn't care less.

"Why did you lie to me about Weston?" she snapped.

"I never lied to you about Weston."

She rolled her eyes so far back in her head she thought they might get stuck there. "You didn't tell me the truth either. You made me think he was a gardener."

Leo didn't flinch or blink. "I did."

Even though she'd already known it was true, it hurt to hear her father admit he'd manipulated her again.

It hurt worse to know Weston was a part of it. Her chest ached every time she thought of that amazing kiss. Now the memory of it was ruined.

"Things are dangerous right now, Kayleigh," Leo continued. "They're only going to get more dangerous and I don't want you getting hurt in the cross fire."

The unspoken *again* made her heartbeat race, but she refused to think about her kidnapping. Fear wouldn't help her get through to her father; it would only convince him that he'd done the right thing by lying to her.

"I know how you feel about Jasper and the rest of the guards, so I thought Weston would be the best way to keep you protected without making you uncomfortable. Evidently, I was wrong."

"Don't do that. This isn't about Weston's ability to protect me, it's about you both lying to me."

As she said it, she realized it was true. Weston had kept her safe and alive when people had come for her. And even before that, she'd felt safe and comfortable. He'd done a great job, but betraying her trust wasn't something she could forgive easily.

"I will do what it takes to keep you safe, Kayleigh. Even if that means I don't always do things you like." Leo rubbed the space between his brows like he had a headache. "But, for the record, Weston thought you knew."

Kayleigh stilled, her heart rate picking up again. "What?"

Leo looked at her again and she could see how tired he was. Bone weary. It hurt to see her father like that even when she was upset with him.

"I told Weston that you agreed to having a bodyguard at the lake house," Leo said. "He went there thinking you already knew he was there to protect you."

Suddenly the conversation on the boat made more sense. Everything made more sense. "And the gardening?"

Leo shrugged. "He mentioned he still liked plants and I told him to feel free to landscape as he wanted to. I even offered to pay extra for it."

Kayleigh felt sick. She'd been so consumed with the imagined betrayal that she never gave Weston a chance to explain. She'd let her father's lies ruin the friendship they'd rekindled.

She'd hurt him.

She had to apologize. But first she had to deal with her father.

She wasn't going to scream. She wasn't going to get hysterical. She calmly walked toward his desk. "Dad, I know you're scared for me and love me, but you can't keep manipulating me like this. I won't tolerate it. I'll see to my own security from now on. Keep your men away from me."

Without waiting for a response, she walked out of his office. She wasn't going to stay in her father's house another minute. Not when she had to find Weston and make things right.

She didn't want him to be her security, but he worked in the business. He'd be able to find or recommend someone.

If he was even willing to talk to her at all after how she'd behaved. She wouldn't blame him if he wanted nothing to do with her.

She made her way to the kitchen to grab her purse and her camera where she'd dropped them earlier, only to find Jasper and Gwendolyn already there.

Gwendolyn took one look at Kayleigh's face and stepped toward her. "What happened?" the older woman asked.

"I'm leaving." Kayleigh gathered her things.

"Whoa, you can't leave." Jasper stiffened. "You were almost kidnapped a few hours ago. It's barely dawn now."

"I can leave and I am. Go talk to your boss. Your services are no longer required when it comes to me."

Jasper stepped forward like he'd grab her, but Gwendolyn held him back with a hand on his arm. "Where are you going?" she asked.

She didn't want to tell them about her plan to apologize. Jasper would throw a fit and she didn't want to deal with it. "I can't stay here. Like I told

Dad, I will handle my own security from now on."

She slid around Jasper, who obviously wasn't sure whether to stop her or not, and headed out to her car, that her father had sent someone to pick up for her. She put Weston's office into her GPS and headed out, trying to think of how she was going to fix things between them.

Weston was important to her. He'd been important all those summers ago and she couldn't deny how important he was becoming to her again, even after just a few days.

She hoped he'd give her a chance.

A glance in the rearview mirror had her groaning at a black SUV a couple vehicles back. Jasper and his team's specialty. It had been there for a while. She wasn't surprised Dad still had someone following her.

Thankfully, her exit was next. So she waited until the very last second to take it, knowing the flow of traffic was too heavy for the SUV to follow. Peeking at the GPS, she found she was only a few minutes away from Weston's office.

She didn't want an audience for this. Especially not Jasper.

They would have a tracker on her vehicle, so she pulled over into a strip mall parking lot. She was only half a mile away. She'd go the rest on foot.

She found a spot quickly and snatched up her purse and camera bag, not wanting to leave them behind. She switched her phone map to walking and headed around the far side of the strip mall.

She hadn't even made it two blocks before she saw Jasper on the other side of the street. Damn it, he'd found her. Thankfully, he was looking in the other direction, so she ducked into an alley to avoid his attention.

She did not want to talk to Jasper. She only wanted to talk to Weston.

She was looking over her shoulder to make sure he wasn't following when something hit her from the opposite direction hard enough to knock her to the ground. The air rushed from her lungs and rough asphalt scraped her arm.

What the hell?

Before she could voice her outrage, a fist crashed into her jaw and everything turned gray.

Chapter Nine

Kayleigh's world swam in the aftermath of the punch. The bricks of the buildings around her blurred as she struggled to breathe, to focus, to get up. Her heartbeat roared in her ear as she rolled to the side. Before she could stumble to her feet, rough hands pushed her into the concrete.

She tried to shake off her panic at being alone and vulnerable in this alley. Was this one of the same people who had come after her at the cabin? How had they found her? Or was it completely random—sheer bad luck?

Either way, she wasn't going down without fighting. Between one breath and the next, she rolled back over and started throwing punches back at her attacker.

She shoved the guy, lashing out, using her arms and legs, yelling at the top of her voice for help. Some landed, some didn't. She could hear him grunting on top of her as her fists connected with him as he tried to cover her mouth so no one could hear her scream.

Her vision swam when he punched her in the jaw again before she could throw up her arms to block it. Between the hits and her frantic movements, she couldn't get a good look at her attacker. Was he wearing a hoodie? She tried blinking through the blurriness, but honestly didn't care if she could see him.

She just wanted to get out of this alley alive.

Finally, a lucky elbow to his face did the job. The body on top of her rolled off. She tried to scramble up and get away, fighting the waves of nausea, but a hand hooked on her ankle and dragged her back, shoving her onto her belly.

She wiggled and screamed, knowing that her advantage was gone and she was vulnerable again. The attacker cursed, yanking the camera bag off her shoulder and wrenching her arm in the process. Kayleigh cried out at the unexpected pain in her shoulder and curled into herself as much as she could, trying to breathe through her pain and terror.

She didn't even realize the attacker was gone until she heard running footsteps getting quieter down the alley.

For a moment, Kayleigh just laid there catching her breath. She rolled over, looking up at the sky.

"I'm alive," she whispered. That was the most important thing, even though everything hurt.

But the bastard had taken her camera.

So this hadn't been a kidnapping attempt, not connected to what had happened at the lake. Just a stupid mugging.

She sat up and did a quick inventory of her body. Her vision was clearing, although her jaw felt puffy and sore. Scrapes on her hands and elbows, but nothing too bad. Even the shoulder pain was already more manageable.

She gritted her teeth at the loss of her camera. It was her favorite, but it could be replaced. She picked up her purse, still on the ground next to her. Mugger would've been smarter to have taken that and gotten the cash and credit card. The camera would be more complicated to fence.

She struggled to her feet. She didn't want to be sitting there hanging out like an idiot if the mugger came to the same realization and decided to return. She leaned against the bricks a couple of times to let dizziness pass then stood and began walking back toward the parking lot.

She'd barely taken a few steps when Jasper and one of his men burst into the alleyway, guns drawn, eyes darting everywhere.

Jasper saw her and ran in her direction. "Are you okay, Miss Delacruz?"

She wanted to tell him he shouldn't even be

there, that she was done with her father's security team, but given the circumstances, that seemed childish.

"I was mugged. The guy stole my camera."

Jasper nodded at the other security team member and the man walked a few steps away and pulled out his phone. No doubt to call the other Jasper clones.

Jasper took a step closer. "We should take you to a hospital."

She shook her head, ignoring the pain it caused. "I don't need a hospital. I got a little knocked around, but it's not too bad."

Jasper looked like he wanted to argue, but was smart enough not to. "Then we should take you home. To your father's house. We can have a doctor come there."

She gritted her teeth again. "I'm on my way to the San Antonio Security office. I need to talk to Weston."

Jasper's jaw tightened at the other man's name. "I don't think seeing him while you are bloody and bruised is a good idea." His tone was much more friendly than the look on his face. "I will make sure someone escorts you to see him later, after you've gotten cleaned up and checked out."

Once again, she wanted to argue, but knew it was childish. She could feel the swelling in her face, her blouse was ripped at the elbow and her palms were bloody. She needed to apologize to Weston but doing it looking like she needed medical assistance was not the best way.

She agreed and Jasper pulled out his phone and called for the car to be brought over.

KAYLEIGH CAUGHT SIGHT of herself in one of the car mirrors on her way back to Leo's house and was glad she'd listened to Jasper. She looked a mess.

By the time they were pulling up to the gates, the adrenaline rush of the attack was gone, leaving her jittery and anxious. Jasper pulled the SUV straight into the garage. Normally he would've let her off at the front, but she was grateful she didn't have to attempt the front steps.

She needed a shower, half a bottle of ibuprofen and industrial-strength makeup to get herself presentable again.

And she needed to talk to Weston. Despite her aches and exhaustion, and horror-movie-victim appearance, there was nothing more important to her than setting things right with him.

That's why when she stepped into the hallway and found him talking with her father—his calm, low voice a balm to her overwrought system—she thought she'd gotten hit harder than she'd figured.

His dark eyes widened when he saw her and he was moving toward her in an instant. "What happened? Are you okay?"

Jasper stepped in front of her. "Back off, Patterson."

"Jasper, get out of the way," Kayleigh snapped, jaw clenched in irritation. But Jasper didn't move. He just stood there like he was the white knight she'd never asked for.

The fact that he felt so strongly about protecting her from the one person she'd ever felt completely safe with was complete irony.

Weston looked him over before taking another step so the two men were shoulder to shoulder.

"A lot of people mistake my quietness for weakness. Don't be one of them. If Kayleigh doesn't want me near her, I will honor her wishes immediately. But until I hear the words from her, get the hell out of my way."

Weston's voice didn't rise; he didn't growl or do anything threatening. But there was danger dripping from every syllable he uttered.

How could she have ever thought he was only a gardener? This man was a warrior.

It was written all over him. Even in jeans and a T-shirt, he looked formidable, and she knew firsthand he had muscles under those clothes to back it up.

"Move, Eeley." If anything, Weston's voice

was a little softer, in complete juxtaposition of his body language.

Kayleigh had no doubt Jasper hated to be told to stand down, but he moved to the side. He shot them both a dirty look before going to stand beside Leo.

Once Jasper was out of the way, Weston wrapped one of his hands gently around her upper arm, the other slid into her hair at the back of her neck. He took in every scrape and bruise.

"I got mugged."

His eyes narrowed. "This close to the kidnapping attempt? Are you sure it was a mugging?"

She shrugged, leaning her head to the side so it rested more fully in his hand. She didn't care that her father or Jasper were watching. It felt so right to lean into Weston's strength.

"It was only one person and he wasn't trying to get me out of the alley. He took my camera."

Weston nodded. "That does sound less like a second kidnapping attempt. Where were you?"

"I was coming to see you. To apologize." She locked eyes with him. "I cut through an alley and got knocked to the ground."

"Looks like you took a couple of hits."

Conceding, she shook her head gingerly. "But it could've been much worse."

Before he could say anything further, Gwendolyn burst into the hall. "Kayleigh, look at you.

Come in the kitchen and sit down. Let's get you some ice."

Weston led her into the kitchen, standing by her side as Gwendolyn tutted over her and rested an ice pack against her cheek. Leo and Jasper followed them in.

"Did you get a look at your assailant?" Weston asked.

"Not really. Everything was blurry, but I think he had a black hoodie on? I don't know for sure."

"That's all right. The important thing is that you're safe," Gwendolyn said, patting Kayleigh's hand. "I'll bring you something soothing to drink."

"This is about the merger," Leo said. She was surprised he'd been quiet for this long. "This is why I said you need protection, Kayleigh."

Here we go again.

"Like I said, Dad, it wasn't a great plan if it was a kidnapping," she argued. "I think it was bad luck."

Leo opened his mouth to speak but Weston beat him to it. "I agree with Kayleigh, Leo. If they were after her specifically, it would've been more than a punch and some minor scrapes. And it would've been more than one person in that alley with her."

Leo frowned. "You may be right, but she needs—"

Kayleigh stopped him before he could go back into her need for a permanent security detail. "I'm okay, Dad. More angry that someone stole my camera than anything else."

Leo walked over and put his hand on her shoulder gently. She patted his hand. "We'll get you a new camera."

She made more than enough money to replace her own camera, especially since it was covered by a robust insurance policy. That reminded her of something they'd insisted on.

"Actually, we may not need to. My insurance company insisted I get a tracker placed on the camera in case I lost it on assignment. We might be able to get it back and find the guy who took it."

"Can you access the tracker on your computer?" Weston asked. "With crimes like this, time is important."

"Yes, I just need a laptop."

Leo tipped his head at Jasper, and the other man left to get one. Gwendolyn reappeared with the tea and Kayleigh sipped it gratefully. She was still exhausted and in desperate need of that shower, but the tea helped a little.

Having Weston here helped most of all.

Jasper returned and handed the laptop to Kayleigh, who quickly typed in the website she needed. Logging into her account, she smiled when she found the tracker still active.

"Here it is," she said, twisting the laptop around so the others could see.

Weston and Jasper both looked at Leo, waiting to see who would be assigned the task. Kayleigh didn't want this to turn into another standoff.

She looked up at Weston. "Can Jasper and his men go get it? I... I'd love for you to stay with me, if you don't mind."

He nodded. "Absolutely."

"We're on it." Jasper took the laptop from her and disappeared out of the kitchen without another word.

"We'll be going, too," Gwendolyn said. "We have business to attend to. Call if you start feeling worse or if you think you need a doctor."

Gwendolyn pulled a protesting Leo from the room. She shoved him out of sight around the corner and gave Kayleigh an exaggerated wink that made her chuckle under her breath.

Finally, she and Weston were alone.

"Why are you here?" she asked. Even if she had made it to his office, she would've missed him.

He gave her a small smile. "I came to apologize. I guess great minds think alike."

"You have nothing to apologize for. Dad tricked both of us. He admitted the truth after you left."

"He wants to keep you safe. I can't fault him for that." The way Weston looked at her, like she was precious to him, made Kayleigh's heart race. "But I'm sorry you felt betrayed. I would never mislead you like that."

She reached up and squeezed his hand that was resting on her shoulder. "I'm sorry I over-reacted and didn't get to the truth before accusing you of something pretty awful."

He smiled. "Let's just call it a reaction to a stressful situation. Besides, now we both know the truth and we can move on."

"You want things to move on between us?"

"I do. Do you?" Weston asked.

"Yeah."

He smiled, lifting one of his hands to caress her cheek gently. His thumb brushed over one of the scrapes, but it didn't hurt.

"It means I'll have to quit working for Leo. That kiss definitely wasn't professional of me. You can no longer be my client."

Kayleigh grinned, leaning closer. "Then you should kiss me again, since I'm not a client."

He didn't say anything else, just tangled his hand into her hair and pulled her closer. Their lips met, and though this kiss was much gentler than the one last night in the lake house kitchen, it was still every bit as passionate.

And this time there were no secrets between them.

Chapter Ten

Twelve hours later, Weston was still at Leo's house. He stood in the kitchen with Leo, Gwendolyn and Jasper, who had finally returned from his search for the stolen camera.

The only one missing was Kayleigh, who was in her second shower of the day. This one hopefully enough to help her to relax and eventually sleep.

Weston hadn't been able to look away from her face and the bruise coloring her cheek this morning as he'd kissed her. Couldn't stop pressing his lips to the scrapes on her skin from where she fell.

It could've been so much worse. There were plenty of muggings that went wrong and someone didn't survive. Kayleigh could have died and he would have lost her before he'd really had her.

Realizing how close it was had made Weston reluctant to leave her side. So, he'd kissed her again. And again. And again.

When her stomach growled, they'd both laughed and pulled away enough to get her some food and some more tea.

He'd sat next to her while she ate, not wanting to be separated yet. When she was done, he'd asked her to go through all the details with him again to be sure she hadn't forgotten or missed something the first time. Then, very gently, had her go through it one more time after that.

He'd been hoping she might remember anything about the perp's face, but didn't press when she didn't. Adrenaline was a crazy thing—it sometimes made certain aspects of an event crystal clear, sometimes blurred it all. Between the adrenaline and the hits she'd taken, she hadn't gotten a look at a face at all.

It was quite interesting to Weston that Jasper and his men had shown up just in the nick of time to be of absolutely no assistance. That wasn't an indication of guilt, but the timing was on the suspicious side.

By the time they'd finished the meal and going through everything, it had been after noon. She'd been blinking slowly and obviously needed to rest. He'd sent her up for her shower, then had been more than happy to hold her while they'd both slept for a few hours.

He'd also called his brothers to have them check out the alley. While San Antonio was certainly a big enough city that there was crime, someone getting mugged midmorning in that part of town wasn't the standard practice.

Beyond that, he'd forced himself to back off. Leo was no longer his boss; Kayleigh wasn't his client to protect.

He'd still be protecting her, but not because it was a job.

By dinnertime, despite the wonderful nap holding Kayleigh safe in his arms, there was no actionable intel. His brothers hadn't found anything usable in the alley. He'd heard Jasper was back from the hunt for the camera but didn't know any details.

He and Kayleigh had a quiet dinner with Gwendolyn. Leo had locked himself in his office and had been on the phone nonstop. Something was up.

Weston had to remind himself it wasn't his responsibility to know everything that was going on. He was here solely as support for Kayleigh.

But when Leo had invited him into his office to hear the report from Jasper, Weston had quickly agreed.

"What happened?" Leo asked Jasper.

"The tracker was a dead end. It took us to a dumpster a couple blocks from the alley where Kayleigh was attacked. But when we got there, no camera, no mugger. We think they removed the tracker."

Weston frowned. "Someone removed a nearly undetectable tracker from Kayleigh's camera and placed it in a dumpster? That's pretty damned lucky."

"I don't know what to tell you, Patterson. The camera wasn't there when we arrived." Jasper's jaw clenched. "You think you could do better?"

Weston didn't say anything. He wasn't going to argue with the other man. But it was quite suspicious that the tracker had led to nothing.

"Let's not worry about the camera." Leo had been pacing in front of the windows in the office the whole time Jasper gave a report, ignoring the tea Gwendolyn brought in for each of them. "It can be replaced. The tracker didn't lead to finding who attacked her, so it's useless. For now, we focus on keeping everyone safe until the merger goes through."

Weston nodded, studying him. Something had happened in the last few hours to agitate the older man. He didn't know if it had to do with what Kayleigh had been through or the merger itself.

He kept an eye on Jasper too. Something was not right about him. He would have his brothers do a full rundown on Jasper to make sure

Leo hadn't missed anything during his background check.

"I want to discuss Kayleigh's safety," Leo said, glancing out the door like Kayleigh might be eavesdropping. "With the mugging and the attack on the lake house, I want her protected at all times."

"I'll take care of it," Weston said immediately, looking at Kayleigh's father. "I have somewhere we can go. But you aren't going to pay me for it."

"Where?" Jasper asked. "Just running off with her isn't a good solution."

Weston wasn't about to tell either man. But especially not Jasper. "She'll be safer if nobody knows."

"That's not going to work." Jasper's neck reddened. "I'm the head of security and I need to know where she is at all times."

"It's not up to you." Weston turned to Leo. "It's not up to you either. This conversation needs to happen with Kayleigh."

He didn't want her to ever again feel like he was keeping secrets about her safety.

"Of course it does." Gwendolyn offered all three men a smile, an attempt at peacekeeping. "But Jasper not knowing where she is could make it difficult to do his job. Whether she likes it or not, he was hired to protect the Delacruz family, and Kayleigh is a huge part of that."

"Kayleigh is a grown woman." Weston crossed his arms over his chest. "She's intelligent and has great instincts. Let her make her own choices."

She was also wary of Jasper. But was that because the man was overbearing and power hungry or because she didn't think he was trustworthy?

Weston saw a flash of movement at the door just before Kayleigh stepped in. She was dressed comfortably in worn jeans and a cozy sweatshirt. Her damp hair was loose around her shoulders, gathering on the backpack she wore.

She looked beautiful and fierce as she stared down her father. "I'm going with Weston. He's the best choice to keep me safe." She patted her backpack as she met Weston's eyes. "I've got everything I need and I'm ready when you are."

Hearing that she trusted him was a balm to his nerves, and as she came over to stand next to him, her closeness soothed him more. She was alive. She was safe.

He would make sure it stayed that way.

"No." Jasper crossed his huge arms over his chest.

"I'm not asking your permission, Jasper. Weston's right. I can make my own choices." Kayleigh turned to Leo. "I need protection, fine. Weston can do that."

"I agree," Leo said. "But I think separating

may not be a good idea. There are things I need to explain about—"

A shrill alarm broke off his argument. Everyone froze, looking at each other, trying to determine what was going on. Weston grabbed Kayleigh's arm and pulled her closer.

Jasper snatched the walkie-talkie from his belt. "Report."

A few seconds later, multiple grainy voices filled the room, talking on top of each other. Weston couldn't make out a lot of what they were saying but one word he definitely understood.

Fire.

Jasper snatched a tablet off the desk and pulled up the security feed.

"Sir, we've got a fire in the east section of the house."

Weston took Kayleigh's hand. The east section of the house was near her bedroom.

"What caused it?" Leo asked.

Jasper rushed to the door. "I'll let you know as soon as I—"

An explosion rocked the room and the windows shattered around the office. Weston spun, wrapping himself around Kayleigh, lowering them both to the floor.

They could hear more explosions and shattering windows all over the property.

They were under attack.

Jasper rushed over to Leo and Gwendolyn and pulled them away from the windows. Reports were screeching from his radio now.

Leo turned to Gwendolyn. "Get all the staff out of the house."

The older woman looked around at them nervously, twisting her hands like she didn't want to go. "But, sir, what about—"

"We'll get out. Jasper, go with her. Do it now!"

Jasper looked like he also wanted to argue, but Leo had already turned away, moving low and quickly toward Weston and Kayleigh.

"Dad, we can't stay here," Kayleigh said, still under Weston's arm. "We need to get out too."

More explosions, and now smoke was filling the hall beyond the door.

"Can you get her out?" Leo asked Weston.

Kayleigh shook her head. "No way. We're not leaving without you."

Leo cupped his daughter's cheeks. "I'll leave, I promise. But I need you to go first. Like you said, Weston will keep you safe. Once I know no one can get to you, I'll do what I need to do."

Kayleigh's safety was more important to Leo than his own. Weston didn't know why, but he would make sure she was protected.

She stared at him, shocked and scared. She'd already had a rough day and he hated it was getting worse. But he was damned well going to get her out.

"Okay," she whispered.

Beside them, Leo deflated, as if hearing her agree had taken the weight of the world off his back. "Good. Thank you."

Gunfire joined the commotion. This was definitely an attack.

"Do you have a plan?" Leo asked.

Weston crept to the door, keeping Kayleigh pinned to his side. "They've blocked everything off, so the garage is the easiest way out, but getting in a car is exactly what they want. So, I'm going to get her out of here by foot."

Leo's gaze was concerned but he agreed. "Okay."

"We're going to go toward the fire." Weston looked at Kayleigh and clutched her hand. "Into the wilderness area behind the house."

Leo reached over and hugged Kayleigh. "Be careful. I love you. I'll get my team to make a distraction so you're sure to get out."

"Be safe," she said, hugging him tight.

"You too." Leo squeezed her once more and let her go, pushing her back to Weston. "Get her out of here."

Weston grabbed Kayleigh again and the two snuck into the back hallway. They pressed themselves to the shadows, using the chaos all around them to their advantage. Multiple guards were rushing toward Leo's office, so he'd at least have protection.

Staying close together, it wasn't long before they made it to the other side of the house where the fire raged. No one had spotted them.

Weston was surprised to see how much damage the flames had already done. Paintings were shredding into ash by the second, expensive wallpaper peeling from the walls. Even away from the direct flames, where they were, the floor tiles cracked from the heat.

Beside him, Kayleigh choked as she looked at the destruction of her childhood home. He grabbed her shirt and pulled it up over her nose, doing the same with his own.

He pointed to a little side door, thankful he still remembered so much of the house from when they were kids. "We're going through that door. Once we're outside, get ready to run. We'll have to jump the back fence."

The property butted up against the Hill Country State Natural Area—no houses, few roads, definitely their best direction for escape.

"Ready?" Weston asked. They were going to have to run through the fire to get out.

She squeezed his hand and nodded. Her trust meant everything to him.

Focusing again, he nicked a throw blanket

from a nearby chair and wrapped it around his hand, moving Kayleigh so that she was farthest from the flames as they approached the door. The air was scorching, making his skin tighten. He reached for the doorknob, feeling the heat through the blanket, but it didn't have time to burn him. Once the door was open, he pushed Kayleigh through and followed, rushing them outside.

Away from the oppressive heat of the fire, the light breeze felt like heaven. They both lowered their shirts off their noses and took a few deep breaths.

Behind them was the sound of more windows breaking and things crashing. He grabbed her hand once more and pulled her toward the back fence, keeping to the shadows. If they were spotted, they'd be in trouble.

Her backpack got stuck as they climbed the fence, so he took it off her back and put it on his own before helping her the rest of the way up and over. He climbed right behind her and jumped to the ground.

They sprinted to the cover of the low trees and then deeper into the surrounding wilderness. If the people attacking were truly trying to get their hands on Kayleigh—no doubt to control Leo—it wouldn't take them long to figure out he and Kayleigh had headed in this direction.

They needed to be long gone before that happened.

Kayleigh ran with Weston like a trouper, staying right beside him despite the punishing pace he set. They weren't nearly as far into the wilderness as he would've liked before his instincts had him stopping and pulling her against a tree.

He covered her mouth with his hand, but quickly let go when he saw terror flash in her eyes dimly lit from the moon. He put his finger over his lips in a signal to remain quiet and she nodded.

He closed his eyes briefly, letting his other senses take over. He didn't hear anything.

At all.

The silence was just as much of a giveaway that there was a problem as bad guys barreling through yelling. More so, because it meant whoever was chasing them was smart enough not to announce it.

A snapping branch to the north snagged his attention. There was definitely at least one person out there. Kayleigh's eyes got wider. She'd heard it too.

A second rustling sound in the opposite direction alerted them to a second adversary.

Weston leaned close to Kayleigh's ear. He spoke in a low tone, knowing that wouldn't carry as far as a whisper. "Remember the grove?"

She nodded. It was a couple miles off the property, but they had gone there a few times with Henry as kids. The trees were bigger there, they'd have more places to hide.

"Stay with me. Step where I do."

She nodded again.

He took her hand, pulling them both into crouches. He moved quickly, aiming for spots of soft wood and moss to cover the sound of their steps. Behind him, Kayleigh did as he'd asked: stepped where he stepped, grabbed where he grabbed.

He knew she had to be scared—it was dark, there was thunder in the distance, and people were chasing them. But she held it together.

And he was going to do whatever he had to do to keep her safe.

Chapter Eleven

"I think they came through here."

Weston pressed his fingers back to his lips as the people tracking them passed close enough for them to hear their whispered words.

As if Kayleigh needed a reminder to be quiet.

Weston's chest brushed hers as he brought his mouth to her ear and it was all she could do not to shiver at his touch.

"Take this." He slipped his phone into her pocket and Kayleigh stilled as his lips grazed her skin. "If anything happens, you run as far and as fast as you can, and then you hide. Find cell service and call any number on speed dial. My brothers will take care of you."

"I don't want to do this without you." She was barely keeping the panic at bay as it was.

He kissed her forehead. "You won't. This is just a contingency plan."

She shook her head, understanding, and Weston turned around to watch the grove again.

He had his gun in his hand and was keeping himself between her and the bad guys—a cedar elm pressed up against her back.

She appreciated his protectiveness, but also didn't want him to get shot trying to save her.

"We'll have to get through him to take her," one voice said, a little closer now.

Kayleigh's stomach dropped.

Visions of her kidnapping flashed through her head. Darkness, the storm. Her jaw ached to make noise, to cry or scream. Anything. But she kept her mouth shut and her breathing quiet.

"I have no problem with that. She's what's important," another voice said.

It felt like the two men were right on top of them. Weston stepped closer, adjusting his stance, making sure she was fully hidden. His frame was steady but tense, ready to move if needed.

"Looks like they came through here, but I can't tell where they went after."

The other guy groaned softly. "This is too much ground to cover just the two of us."

Only two of them was a good thing.

"We keep looking. I'll call for backup."

The other man grumbled but didn't object. Soon the footsteps and voices faded away into nothingness, leaving only the whisper of the wind through the trees and bushes.

The silence stretched on as Kayleigh counted the seconds, wanting to move, but Weston stayed still. It was nearly five minutes before Weston's body finally relaxed.

"I wanted to make sure they weren't trying to draw us out," he said, voice still low. "But they're gone."

"How do you know?"

"The wildlife started chatting with each other again."

She cocked her head and, sure enough, could hear the night sounds of crickets and other small animals.

He turned to her, taking her hand. "Doing okay?"

She bobbed her head. She wasn't great—exhaustion was starting to really beat down on her—but they were alive. That was the most important thing. "Where are we going?"

"We'll follow the river for a while. If memory serves, that will lead us to one of the access roads. I want to get as far away from the house as possible since it sounded like they'll have reinforcements coming in."

Kayleigh's mouth dried at the thought of an entire team of people scouring the area for them. Two had been bad enough.

She followed Weston as he took the lead, still stepping where he did in case it would help.

Once they made it to the river, she had to ask what was on her mind. "Do you think my dad is okay?"

He sighed. "Honestly, I don't know. He has measures in place so that his death doesn't stop the merger."

Kayleigh shouldn't be surprised Leo had done that. Business had always been the most important thing to him. "Hopefully that's enough to keep him safe."

"I would've thought so but…"

Something in Weston's voice dug at her. "What? What aren't you telling me?"

He stopped and turned to look at her. "There's no concrete evidence, but I think whoever is after you is closer than we think."

"Why do you say that?"

"Between the lake house, which no one knew about, the mugging and the fire, it's too much of a coincidence." He must have seen the panic on her face because he stepped closer and ran his hands down her arms. "Like I said, I don't know for sure, but I don't believe in coincidences."

"You think someone in Dad's inner circle is behind this."

"Either that or giving away information to people they shouldn't. Regardless, they've found you too easily each time. I don't like it."

Her mind whirled as she thought through all

the staff members who could've possibly gone turncoat on her father. There were dozens who worked at the house. "We have to tell Dad."

"He's probably already figured it out, but I'll call as soon as we get service. Let's get going."

Weston held out his hand and Kayleigh didn't hesitate to take it. She needed the touch to ground herself as much as she did to know where she was going. Everything had become a lot more complicated.

The worry in her mind turned off after another couple of hours of rushing through the wilderness. It was taking all her focus just to keep her body going.

Weston helped or she wouldn't have made it. He was a pro at finding the flattest path through the trees. He gave warnings about low branches or tripping roots. But it was still brutal.

Then the skies opened up with the storm that had been blowing nearer all night and poured. Fear skittered down her spine as the first sounds of thunder rolled through the air. She fought the panic. There wasn't time for it.

She wished it was that easy to turn off.

Weston looked over, his hand squeezing hers gently. It reminded her that she wasn't alone, wasn't a trapped, helpless child.

Fifteen minutes later, they were both soaked.

Wet, even on a mild spring Texas night, was still chilly.

"Can I get my jacket out of my backpack?" She'd thrown a few things in there with her camera since she thought they'd be leaving Leo's house.

This wasn't what she'd been expecting.

He stopped and she got the jacket out of the bag.

"What else do you have in there?" Weston asked as she finally pulled the jacket free.

"Nothing that'll fit you, unfortunately. A change of clothes, toothbrush, toothpaste, deodorant, a brush and...my film camera." Kayleigh felt her cheeks warm. "Sorry that you're having to carry all this stuff. Should we just ditch it?"

She hated the thought of losing the camera she'd owned for so long but knew she needed to keep her priorities straight.

"It's not slowing me down. Believe me, I carried much heavier packs than this when I was in the military."

He could probably carry her all the way out of here if he needed to. Thunder boomed over them and she clenched her teeth and forced herself to breathe, hoping she wasn't going to have to find out if that was the case or not.

She would *not* be a burden to him.

"We need to find shelter before this gets worse," he said.

She wasn't sure if he wanted to do that because he knew how panicked she was or because the nature reserve tended to flood. It didn't matter. They started their trek again, and while Weston looked for shelter, Kayleigh checked the phones whenever they stopped for cover. Each time she hoped to see service bars on the screen, but nothing came. She wasn't surprised. This area was known for no signal.

By the time Weston found an overhang that would work to protect them from most of the storm, they were both close to shivering. Thankfully, they'd heard no signs of pursuit from the men after them, and Weston reassured her that whatever trail they left would be untraceable with the rain.

"Come on. Let's get you out of those wet clothes and into something warm."

The little space, about halfway up a small canyon, was barely big enough for them both to lie down in, but it at least protected them from the weather.

She crawled in, stripped out of her jacket and laid it out. "What about you? You don't have anything to change into." She wasn't sure if it would really dry all that much but figured it wouldn't hurt to try. Once she was changed, she turned back to Weston. "Oh."

He'd stripped out of his shirt and unbuttoned his pants, though he kept them on before dropping to sit on the ground. Kayleigh was having trouble figuring out exactly where to look. His muscular arms, his toned stomach, his long fingers.

It wasn't fear that had her resenting the dark now; it was her inability to see him fully.

He took her hand and pulled her down next to him. "You should try to get some sleep. We can't start a fire, but hopefully if we stay close together, we'll be warm enough."

Kayleigh was about to decline, reminding him about her issues with storms, but he wrapped his arm around her and pulled her head onto his chest. She went willingly, laying her ear over his heart. The rhythmic thumping soothed her, reminded her that they were alive and together. And while she could still feel the anxiety from the storm and surrounding darkness pressing on her, it was enough to keep it at bay.

Clinging to Weston with an arm around his waist, Kayleigh let her eyes close. She still wasn't sure how the boy she'd known had turned into the fierce man in front of her, one who had kept her safe in multiple situations now, but she was grateful.

This overhang may be providing them shelter from the physical storm, but he was her shelter from all the other ones.

WESTON DIDN'T SLEEP, but he didn't mind that a bit. Even though his back ached from the position he'd been in all night, he couldn't force himself to wake Kayleigh.

She seemed so peaceful in his arms, her warm breath skittering across his chest with every exhale. He wished the circumstances were different and they were in his bed together. That he could wake her up with a promise of pleasure that would have them both forgetting their own names.

Instead, waking her now would push her straight back into a nightmare. She needed rest because he was afraid the worst part of all of this was still in front of them. The storm may have passed but they had other things to face down.

His mind whirled as the darkness faded into early morning twilight. Whoever was behind this was definitely somebody with inside knowledge of Leo's network. Weston's money was on Jasper. Something about him had never sat right. But it could be any of the security team. Hell, any of Leo's staff altogether.

His lawyer, Dean McClintock, was privileged to all Leo's inside info—Leo had spent most of the day with him yesterday. Hell, even Gwendolyn couldn't be discounted.

He needed to get Kayleigh back to civilization and figure out who they could trust.

As much as he hated to do so, he gently shifted once there was full light and woke the beautiful woman lying on him. She shifted then blinked those green eyes at him as it all came back to her.

"Are we safe?" she whispered. "I can't believe I slept."

"The storm is gone and there's been no sign of any bad guys after us. But we need to get moving. We'll need to find somewhere with service."

She looked away, the tips of her ears turning red as her stomach growled loudly enough to be heard. "And to get something to eat."

Weston laughed, though he wasn't much better off. All he wanted was a bottle of water and a burger. "Let's get moving then."

As they left the overhang, he checked for signs of anyone else having been near them and didn't find any. That didn't mean they were out of danger, but they wouldn't have to set such a grueling pace.

Still, time wasn't on their side. They made their way through the trees, enjoying the warmth that the slow sunrise brought them. It wasn't much, but after a wet night outside, it was at least something. After an hour of brisk walking, Kayleigh never complaining despite the damp clothes and growling stomach, Weston's phone had service.

He immediately called his brothers.

"San Antonio Security, this is Chance."

Weston didn't even ask why Maci wasn't answering the phone. If Chance had killed her, Weston didn't want to know about it. "Chance, it's me."

"Thank God, Weston. Where the hell are you? Do you know Leo Delacruz's place burned down last night?"

"Yeah, we were there. Kayleigh and I had to take off into the public wilderness area behind the house and hide out. Someone is after her."

Chance muttered a curse. "You okay? What do you need?"

"We're all right, but we could use a ride. Water, food. We just spent the night in the nature reserve and we're both a little worse for wear."

"Injuries?"

"None," Weston replied.

"Good. Where are you?"

Weston pulled up the GPS app on his phone and rattled off an area of the road a bit farther off their path to Chance.

"I'll be there in thirty minutes," his brother promised. "Stay safe."

"We will." Weston disconnected the call and

turned to Kayleigh. "My brother Chance is on his way."

"Can I call my dad?"

He hated to disappoint her but it was too dangerous. "We can't. Not yet. If this is an inside job, like we're thinking, Leo's phone may be monitored. We can't take a chance on leading anybody to us."

Her lips tightened, but she nodded.

He hooked a hand at the back of her neck and trailed his thumb down her cheek. "Let's get somewhere safe, then contacting your dad will be top of the list of things to do."

"Okay," she whispered.

He led them the rest of the way to the rendezvous point, keeping them both in the shadows of a group of trees until Chance pulled up.

"All good?" he asked.

Weston helped Kayleigh into the back seat and climbed in next to her. Chance tossed back some water bottles and granola bars, as well as a blanket.

"Yeah, thanks for the lift. Spot anything suspicious coming out?"

He met his brother's eyes in the rearview mirror. "No. Luke was coming in from the other direction to make sure there were no problems. Brax is tailing me about a mile behind."

Weston nodded and tore into one of the water bottles as Kayleigh devoured a nutrition bar.

"Kayleigh, I'd like you to meet my brother Chance. Chance, Kayleigh Delacruz."

Chance held a hand up in a friendly wave. "Nice to meet you. Sorry Weston hasn't learned that showing a lady a good time doesn't have to include wilderness survival training."

Kayleigh smiled. "Our next date will involve no running through the wilderness."

Their next date. Weston was determined there would be one.

Hell, there would be hundreds.

"I hate to be the bearer of bad news…" Chance continued. "We got more intel about the fire, and it's not good."

Kayleigh stiffened. "Oh God."

"No fatalities, but there were some injuries. Kayleigh…your father is in the hospital. I don't know much but—"

She turned to Weston. "We have to go. I have to see him."

"That's exactly where they'll expect you to go," Chance said.

"I don't care. If it was one of your parents, would you hide and wait for word or would you be there?"

Weston didn't even have to consult his brother. There was no way in hell any of the Patterson boys wouldn't be at their parents' side in that situation.

That didn't mean he liked bringing Kayleigh into danger. He let out a sigh. "It's not the safest plan."

She narrowed her eyes. "You'll keep me safe. But we're going."

He gave her a short nod then got out his phone. He would need to set things in motion with his brothers to make sure she was truly secure.

"Okay. We go."

He reached over and grabbed her hand. She squeezed it, relief clear on her features.

He hoped he wasn't making a huge mistake.

Chapter Twelve

Weston was right on Kayleigh's heels as she burst through the hospital's waiting room door. Chance had entered first to scope out the situation and make sure there were no immediate threats. Weston wasn't sure where Luke and Brax were, but knew they were also already in the building.

Upon arrival, a front-desk attendant escorted him and Kayleigh to a private section of the hospital. The waiting room was like any other hospital—beige walls, white-tiled floors and uncomfortable chairs.

Everyone inside the room was part of Leo's employment. Under other circumstances that would've made Weston more comfortable, but not today.

The door hadn't even closed behind them when Gwendolyn threw herself at Kayleigh with a relieved sob. Weston curbed the reflex to pull Kayleigh away from the incoming hug—potential danger—but stayed close.

"Thank God, you're okay," Gwendolyn whispered.

"You?" Kayleigh asked. "Are you hurt?"

"No, I'm fine."

Kayleigh captured the other woman's hands. "How is Dad?"

Weston hated how Kayleigh's lip quivered and whole body shook with fine tremors. He took her by the arm and gently led her toward the chairs to sit next to him while Chance stood guard nearby.

The older woman cleared her throat, but before she could answer, someone else did. "Not well. Coma. They wouldn't tell us more until you got here."

"Dean! Your bedside manner is terrible." Gwendolyn scolded the lawyer before turning back to Kayleigh. "I'll let the nurses know you're here. We're hoping Leo's doctor will be out shortly with an update."

Kayleigh looked over at Weston. "I need to know what's happening. I need to see him."

"You will," Weston soothed. He looked around and realized they were missing a major player in Leo's forces. "Where's Jasper?"

"Stayed behind to see who started the fire," one of the security guards said.

Weston caught Chance's eye. The head of security leaving his client alone in the hospital after an attack that large? That didn't sit right.

Someone needed to ensure Leo's safety. "How many guards on Leo's door?"

"Two."

Weston nodded. A smaller team made it harder to keep a client safe in times of chaos, but was also harder to infiltrate. The bigger problem was that Weston had no idea which of Leo's— or, more accurately, Jasper's—men could be trusted.

Weston and Chance shared another look and he knew his brother was thinking the same thing. They'd have to sort out security for Leo on their own.

Before he could ask any more questions, Gwendolyn came back with a doctor just behind her.

"Kayleigh Delacruz?"

Kayleigh jumped up and rushed toward the man. "That's me. How is my father?"

"I'm Dr. Appleton, your father's personal physician."

When she shook his hand, Appleton gave her a typical doctor smile, friendly without making promises or offering hope. It sent something cold slithering through Weston's stomach to see it. Smiles like that tended to be bad news.

From the way Kayleigh's smile stiffened, she had the same thought.

"I'll be frank with you. Your father is in a coma and we can't figure out why. At first, we thought it was from smoke inhalation, but his lungs are improving consistently and there's no sign of any internal damage besides that. Smoke inhalation isn't consistent with a coma anyway."

"So what does that mean?" Kayleigh asked, reaching for Weston's hand and gripping it like it was a lifeline. He smoothed his thumb over her skin in gentle circles, trying to give her a piece of the calm she so desperately needed.

"It means there's nothing we can do right now except wait. We'll monitor him round the clock and keep looking for the cause of his coma. But without it, there's not a lot we can do."

Kayleigh was quiet. The tightness of her hand in Weston's was the only indicator that she'd even heard the doctor. When she spoke, her voice was hoarse and thick. "I want to see him."

"Of course. Right this way. We just ask that there is only one person in with him at a time. And only people you approve."

"Okay."

"Actually, Kayleigh, I'd like to speak with you before you go see Leo," Dean said. "I know it's bad timing, but I wouldn't ask if it wasn't urgent."

Kayleigh blew out an exasperated breath, saying, "Gwendolyn, you go in first. We'll trade out once I'm through here."

"I'll go back in just a minute." She pulled Kayleigh in for another hug, shooting another ugly look at Dean, obviously afraid the man was going to be insensitive again. "I'm here for you, Kayleigh. Whatever you need."

Dean smoothed the jacket of his suit, pressing out invisible creases before he turned to Kayleigh. "I need to know what your father told you about the Brighton Pharmaceuticals merger."

"Can't this wait, Dean?" Gwendolyn asked.

"It's important," the man muttered. "I need to know what Leo told you about the merger."

Kayleigh's eyes narrowed, but when she spoke, her voice was low and controlled. "My father is lying in a hospital bed in a coma and you're asking me about a merger? I've never had anything to do with my father's business dealings and I certainly didn't start now."

Dean sighed. "I promise, I'm not trying to upset you, but I need to get to the bottom of things." He looked around the room and Weston could practically see him composing his speech in his head. "This merger has always been strange. Different than all the rest."

"How so?" Weston asked. He kept a casual

eye on the others in the room to see if anyone was reacting in a strange way.

"It's different in that I don't know much about it."

Kayleigh crossed her arms over her chest. "Why would Dad keep you out of the loop?"

Dean stroked his chin. "I've been at Leo's side since his business was barely off the ground. I've been through plenty of mergers with him and this is only the second time he's actively kept details from me."

"What was the first?" Kayleigh asked.

"When Leo bought out George Kesler's business five years ago."

Kayleigh's eyes got a little bigger. "I remember that. He was Dad's rival."

Weston glanced over at Chance and saw him texting. No doubt he was having Maci dig up anything she could on George Kesler.

Gwendolyn bobbed her head. "He and Leo were enemies."

Dean nodded. "Kesler's bread and butter was medical research and artificial intelligence. Leo saw an opportunity and bought Kesler's company. He was supposed to sell it as a whole, but something changed."

"Changed how?" Weston asked.

Dean's jaw got tighter. "It was the meeting I wasn't invited to. Leo and Kesler went into the meeting together. I don't know what happened, but afterward, Leo was the owner and he dismantled Kesler's entire business. Everything sold off in pieces."

Gwendolyn crossed her arms over her chest. "That was before my time, but Leo has mentioned it. Are you sure this needs to be discussed right now, Dean? Kayleigh wants to get in to see Leo."

Kayleigh shook her head. "Do you think Kesler is behind the attack on Dad and kidnapping attempts? Some sort of revenge?"

"He can't be," Dean responded. "A few months after the merger was finished, he had a heart attack and died."

Gwendolyn gasped, hand flying to her mouth. "Oh my gosh."

Kayleigh let out a sigh. "I'm sorry to hear that and even sorrier if Dad's actions had a part in the heart attack cause. But what does this have to do with now?"

"Because this current merger Leo has been so worried about involves George Kesler's son, Beau."

Dean took some papers out of his briefcase and handed them around. One was a picture of Beau, the others images and data about Brighton Pharmaceuticals.

Weston's eyes narrowed. "So, Leo's involved

with another Kesler, he's keeping secrets from you, and there have been multiple attacks against him and Kayleigh."

None of those things individually were good. All three together were very bad.

Dean nodded. "Yes. Beau built Brighton Pharmaceuticals after his father died."

Weston looked over at Gwendolyn. "Do you know anything more than Dean about the merger? Has Beau attempted to contact Leo or come by the house?"

"No. I've never seen Beau Kesler in my life. Leo has kept me out of the loop about a lot of this merger too."

"It's in three days," Kayleigh whispered. "What happens with it if Dad's still in a coma?"

"All of Leo's mergers have a clause in it that require them to continue to completion once they've started." Dean's eyes darted between Kayleigh and Weston. "So, no matter what happens, the merger will go forward. In cases like this where Leo is unavailable due to medical issues, I have power of attorney, but I'll need your signature too."

"Fine, whatever," Kayleigh said. "I just want to see my father."

"Then that's what we'll do. Leave her alone for a while, Dean." Gwendolyn slid an arm around

Kayleigh. They made their way to the door and were quickly whisked away by a nurse.

Weston itched to follow after them. He wanted his own eyes on Kayleigh, especially since everyone else was a potential suspect. He stood, ready to do just that when Dean's voice called him back.

"Weston, there's something else," Dean said, eyes darting to the door Kayleigh just disappeared through before settling back on Weston. "Leo has another clause in his contracts. In the case of his incapacitation or death, Kayleigh has the authority to halt or continue any merger at her discretion."

He raised an eyebrow. "She can override everything? So she'll have sole decision-making power for whether the merger goes through or not."

"Yes."

Weston's stomach tightened and he looked over at Chance, who was still standing at the door, lips now pursed. He was thinking the same thing. Kayleigh was in more danger than they'd realized.

"You need to take her somewhere safe," Dean said. "If someone's trying to make sure the merger doesn't go through, she's the target now."

"Beau Kesler?"

Dean shook his head. "I don't think it's him.

Beau will be making a lot of money in this merger. It's not in his best interest to stop it."

Chance took a step closer. "We've been doing some digging into the merger since Weston took the case. What about Oliver Lyle?"

"Lyle? I know him," Dean responded. "He's a competitor in the medical research sector."

"Of all the interested parties surrounding this merger, Lyle is the most alarming. He's never been arrested, but there are rumors he's used force to seal some lucrative deals for his company in the past. Whispers that he's not above shaking someone down to get a signature, or stop one."

Weston gritted his teeth. This wasn't good. "How does this merger affect him directly?"

"Brighton Pharmaceuticals is a direct competitor," Dean said. "If Leo buys the company and raises it to the top of the industry like he has every other company he's taken over, Lyle could lose everything."

The more Weston learned, the more the need to keep Kayleigh close and safe beat at him. Even knowing she was down the hall was almost too far for him. He couldn't see her. Couldn't feel her presence. And it made him anxious.

Dean's phone rang and he stepped away to answer it with a polite nod. Weston glanced at Jasper's men by the doors and caught his brother's eye, tipping his head to bring Chance closer. They had a window of time without anyone else around and he intended to use it.

"Knowing who could be behind the attacks is one thing, but right now we need to figure out how to keep Kayleigh and Leo safe," he said in barely above a whisper. "Leo's security team can't be trusted."

Chance looked over at the other men. "Agreed. You said you have an idea of where to take Kayleigh?"

Weston sighed, dragging a hand over his face. He was exhausted, but there would be no rest anytime soon. Not until Kayleigh was somewhere no one would find them. "I do, but getting her to leave is going to be a problem."

"What are you going to tell her?"

"The truth." No way was he about to start lying to her now. "She knows Leo's already compromised. Someone on the inside is working against him."

"So we use one of our teams?"

The guards across the room shifted. Weston knew they couldn't hear, but he turned so his back was to them, to make sure neither of them was attempting to figure out their conversation by reading lips.

"I don't even trust this to one of our teams.

I want family-only on this." Kayleigh was too important.

"Pulling out the big guns, aren't you, brother?"

"She's worth it."

Chance didn't even tease him, just offered a nod. "All right then. Family only. Luke, Brax and I can take turns here, but we'll need a few other guys to help out or we'll be spread too thin if something happens."

"Agreed. Pick the ones we trust implicitly and make sure everyone keeps the mission to themselves. We need to keep this quiet."

Chance opened his mouth but before he could say anything, the door opened behind them. Weston spun around to find Jasper striding through the door with two more of his men.

As soon as Jasper saw Weston, his face pinched and he scowled. "What are you doing here?"

Weston kept calm and focused. "Watching over Kayleigh and Leo. Where have you been, Jasper?"

"Trying to figure out what happened at the house."

"And you thought that was more important than staying with Leo yourself? You left your client alone in a hospital bed. What kind of security does that?"

Jasper's hands clenched at his sides and he

took a step toward Weston. "How dare you insinuate that I don't care about my job. I was out there trying to figure out who is after Leo. What have you been doing? Rolling around in the mud with Kayleigh?"

Weston curbed the urge to react to the other man's blatant disrespect of Kayleigh. "If that's how you speak about your boss's daughter, then you aren't the right person to protect either of them. I think it's time for you to take some time off. Your services are no longer required. Once Leo is awake, you can take it up with him."

"I don't work for you, Patterson," Jasper snarled. "I'm the head of Delacruz security. That includes your precious Kayleigh. So, if anything, you work for me."

Weston stepped forward, only to have Chance pull him back. His brother didn't have to say anything; this wasn't the time or place to get into a physical altercation.

Dean, finally finished with his phone call, joined them, and Weston could see the stone-cold lawyer in him. "Technically, Jasper, Leo has it set up so you work for *me* until he wakes up. I'm finding I agree with Weston. We're in the middle of a crisis and your priorities are obviously more focused on proving you're the best person for the job instead of actually protecting Leo. We don't have room in this mess for your fragile ego. Until things have settled, you and your men are on leave."

Jasper's face reddened, from his neck to the tips of his ears, and Weston steeled himself.

"You're going to regret this." Jasper spun on his heel, jerking his head for the others to follow him.

That was one problem settled, but not the biggest one by a long shot.

"I'll contact Brax and Luke, and get a schedule sorted out," Chance said.

Weston nodded. "I'm going to see Kayleigh." He held his hand out to Dean and the two men shook as Chance walked to the corner of the room with his phone. "Thanks for your help with that."

"No thanks needed. My job is to protect Leo's interests and Jasper didn't have them at heart. Not the right ones anyway." He dug into his briefcase and pulled out a business card, handing it to Weston. "Take this. Call if you need anything."

Weston agreed, though he doubted he'd use it. Dean wouldn't be able to help them where they were going. He took out his wallet and slipped the card in, removing one of his own for the lawyer. "We'll be out of cell service, but if you need to contact us, you can call the office. My brothers will know how to get in touch."

Dean took the card and slipped it into his pocket before resting a hand on Weston's shoulder. "I know it's only three days, but keep her safe. Leo won't cope well if anything happens to Kayleigh again."

"I'll protect her with my life."

It was his job, putting his client's safety first, but Weston found that, for the first time ever, he meant more than that. He knew without hesitation he'd do anything to keep Kayleigh alive and well. He just had to hope that it wouldn't come to that.

Chapter Thirteen

Kayleigh watched the lines of her father's heart monitor, both of her hands wrapped around one of his like a lifeline. The *beep, beep, beep* acted as white noise as she struggled to reconcile the larger-than-life man she'd always known with the one lying in the hospital bed in front of her.

She'd never seen him so *still*. Kayleigh couldn't remember the last time she'd seen him rest during the day. Had he ever? She doubted it. There was always business to do, deals to be made.

"I'll rest when I'm dead," he'd always told her.

She desperately didn't want it to come to that anytime soon.

She ran her hand over his arm and frowned at the coolness of his skin. Maybe he was cold and couldn't tell them. She was about to ask Gwendolyn to find another blanket when she remembered the other woman had stepped out to grab coffee. She got up to dig through the cabinets herself, finally finding an extra blanket to lay over her father. She hoped it made him more comfortable because the scratchy fabric certainly didn't make her feel any better.

Kayleigh hated hospitals.

For places meant to keep people alive, there was no life between their walls. It was unnerving. Even in this private section of the hospital only afforded to those who didn't mind paying the exorbitant amount that insurance wouldn't cover, she felt uneasy.

It reminded her of her mother's stay in a hospital just like this when she'd gotten sick. No matter how good the doctors were, or how exclusive the suite, it sometimes didn't matter and people died.

Sitting next to her father, she was afraid if she looked away from him for a second, she'd lose him like she had her mother. Even knowing the stress and exhaustion of the past thirty-six hours were playing a huge role in the despair circling her, tears were still rimming her eyes.

Get it together. Dad's safe here and he's going to be okay. Now is not the time to have a breakdown.

She kept repeating the words to herself, hoping that if she heard them enough, it would make it real.

The door pushed open. "You guys doing okay?"

She rushed into Weston's arms before she could stop herself, thankful when he caught her and tugged her against his chest. Having him here, surrounding her with his warmth and support, was enough to pull her out of the worst of her fears.

Weston wasn't going to let anything happen to her or her father.

He kissed the top of her head. "Any change?"

"Nothing. He's so still. I hate it."

Weston released a small sigh. "You're not going to like this, but we need to get you out of here."

"I don't want to leave him." She pulled back.

He gave her a little bit of space, but kept his hands gently on her arms. "If it were safe, I'd guard the door for you day and night so you didn't have to leave, but staying puts you both at risk."

"Why?"

"Dean told us about another clause in your father's contracts that gives you the power to stop the merger if anything happens to him."

She stiffened, the room feeling even more cold than it had been before. "That's why they're after me."

"Now that Leo's in a coma, they'll come for you even harder. Staying here makes you both easier targets."

She knew he was right, but her father wasn't safe alone. "We can't leave him here unprotected."

"We won't. My brothers will take turns watching over him." He ran his thumbs up and down her arms. "I'm not letting anyone I don't trust with my life near you or your father."

It shouldn't have meant so much to her, but hearing Weston's conviction, seeing it in his face, was enough to soothe the very worst aches in her heart. "What about Jasper and his team?"

"Since we don't know who we can trust, they've been temporarily removed from your dad's service. Leo can sort it out when this is all over."

She was about to voice her relief at that decision when there was another knock on the door. She thought it would be Gwendolyn returning, but it was Dr. Appleton.

"We have everything set up like you asked, Mr. Patterson. Your security team will be the only ones given access to this room."

Weston nodded. "Good."

"We'll do everything we can to keep Mr. Delacruz safe. Security is aware of what's going on and they'll add an additional layer of protection while he's here." The doctor turned to Kayleigh. "I'll keep you updated with his progress, as well."

There was nothing else to ask. Her father would be safe and well cared for. All she had to do was agree.

It was still hard to leave him.

She crossed over to the bed and pressed a kiss to her father's forehead. She couldn't figure out how to tell him what she needed to say.

Don't leave me.

I need you.

I love you.

She couldn't say any of it. Instead she whispered, "Rest easy and wake up soon."

She straightened, holding back the tears threatening to spill, and prayed this wasn't the last time she saw him alive. No matter their differences, she didn't want to live in a world where Leo Delacruz didn't exist.

Warm fingers wrapped around hers and she clung to Weston's hand like a lifeline.

"Let's go," she told him, nodding to the doctor.

Chance was waiting just outside the door.

"I packed the car the best I could. You've got plenty to keep you going until this is over." He tossed his keys to Weston before smiling at Kayleigh. "We're going to keep your dad safe, okay? I promise."

She nodded, praying it was true. "Thank you."

"Anything for family," he said, winking at her.

Kayleigh didn't have it in her to laugh with him, but she tried to at least smile. "Be safe."

"We will. Update when you can." Weston clasped her hand and led her into the elevator. As soon as the doors closed, he pulled out his phone and sent a quick text message.

"Where are we going?" Exhaustion had her nearly swaying on her feet.

"Somewhere safe. I'd rather not tell you yet, if that's okay."

"You know what? I don't even care where we go as long as I can take a shower."

Weston chuckled and pulled her tight against his side. "I'm pretty sure that's something we can manage."

KAYLEIGH STARED OUT the window as Weston drove, though her eyes were mostly unfocused. They pulled up to a stop sign. "Haven't we already come this way?"

He reached over and gave her hand a quick squeeze. "Yeah. But I want to make sure we have no tails before we head to the house."

When he said "house," she assumed he meant some sort of safe house. And although she wasn't entirely sure what she envisioned by "safe house," it definitely wasn't a cute little two-story Spanish Colonial on the outskirts of San Antonio.

"Is this your house?" she asked, noting the beautiful garden in the front. The landscaping definitely seemed his style.

"It was at one point." They parked, and he led her around to the rear of the house with a hand on her back. "Let's get inside as quietly as possible."

Kayleigh didn't understand why they were sneaking in, but it didn't matter. She could practically feel the shower calling. They stepped through the sliding-glass door on the back deck and crept up the staircase.

They went inside a room that had a small desk, twin bed and posters of basketball players on the wall.

"This will be you. Bathroom's through that door." He pointed to the first door in the hallway. "There should be some clean clothes on the counter that will be close enough to fitting you. Take your shower and we'll go downstairs."

The more she looked around, the more she realized she was standing in a teenage boy's room.

Not just any teenage boy. *Weston* teenage boy.

"Where are we, Weston?"

"My parents' place. Clinton and Sheila Patterson's house."

He'd talked about his parents and his siblings, but Kayleigh had never expected to be in their home.

"And the clothes?"

"I texted Brax. You and his wife, Tessa, are about the same size, so I had him drop off something for you to wear."

"Thank you." She hesitated. "Are you sure it's a good idea that I'm here?"

Weston pulled her in for a hug. "I wouldn't have brought you here if I didn't think you were safe."

That wasn't exactly what she was worried about, but now that he mentioned it… "I'm a dangerous houseguest to have right now."

He shrugged. "Does this look like a place people will assume Kayleigh Delacruz is hiding?"

Kayleigh looked around the room with its lace curtains and comfortably worn bedspread. It looked homey and comfortable and, even though she liked it, she saw Weston's point. "No."

He winked at her. "Enjoy your shower."

As soon as the door closed behind him, Kayleigh rushed into the bathroom and stayed in the spray until her fingers wrinkled. The water washed away the grime and dirt from their wilderness trek, but couldn't do much about her worry.

Clean and dressed again, she stepped into the hallway and found Weston waiting for her. "Ready to head down?"

She could hear multiple people talking downstairs so it was obviously more than merely Sheila and Clinton in the house.

Kayleigh smiled thinly. "Are you sure it's okay?"

"Absolutely." His grin was so big she couldn't help but smile back.

Weston led the way down the stairs and into the kitchen. Kayleigh took it all in before they were noticed. The two men—an older Black man and a younger man of mixed race—cooed at the baby who toddled around the kitchen table, holding on to their fingers.

The two women, an older Latina woman who must be Sheila, and a younger white woman who looked just like the baby, were huddled over the counter, preparing food and chatting.

The kitchen was small, not even a third of the size of the kitchen at Leo's house. But there was so much life in this room. So much love.

Kayleigh couldn't recall there ever being this much affectionate chaos going on around her. She just wanted to bask in it.

"That's my brother Brax and my dad, Clinton, playing with little Walker." The toddler let out the most adorable laugh right at that second. "Walker is Brax's son/nephew."

Her brow creased. "Uh…"

Weston tapped her on the nose with a smile. "Biological nephew but son by love and marriage. Families get built in all sorts of crazy ways. We don't question it around here."

Sheila's eyes lit up when she saw Weston. She wiped her hands off and rushed in for a hug. "Weston, I didn't know you were here yet."

"We snuck in the back. Needed to shower and change before we came down." He smiled and kissed her on the cheek before turning back to Kayleigh and drawing her forward. "Everyone, this is Kayleigh Delacruz."

Weston made quick introductions and Sheila immediately swept her up into a hug. For a moment, Kayleigh could barely move. She hadn't had a motherly hug from anyone but Gwendolyn in ages and she'd forgotten how good it felt.

And the fact that this woman loved Weston so much made it feel even better.

"You're a photographer, right?" Sheila asked as she scooted back.

Kayleigh nodded.

"I thought so. I've seen some of your pictures. Well, come on in and help yourself. If you want, you can help us finish up dinner. We're making everyone's favorites. You look half starved, so I'll even look the other way if you want to sample things while we cook." Sheila walked over to the counter.

"You don't have to, if you aren't up for it," Weston whispered.

Kayleigh smiled. "I don't mind."

"I just don't want you to feel pressured."

"No one's pressuring anyone," Sheila said, waving a towel at her son. "Honestly, Weston, you make it sound like I'm yanking her around by the belt loops."

Weston seemed to quickly understand that he wasn't going to win and stepped over the table to play with his nephew with his dad and brother.

Sheila and Tessa worked together on dinner with an ease that spoke of how close they were. Each of them had their own jobs and knew exactly what to do.

Kayleigh wasn't a great cook but neither woman seemed to mind. They gave her jobs that suited her and corrected her with kindly teasing smiles when she made a mistake.

Everybody laughed and talked all over each other. The men set the table and constantly tried to sneak food. Everyone stopped to coo over Walker every few minutes, and the fifteen-month-old ate it up, blowing bubbly kisses to everyone.

Dinner was the opposite of the norm of family meals she'd experienced. Nothing here was formal and definitely not quiet and refined. It was overwhelming, but Kayleigh loved it.

After the meal, Weston and Kayleigh insisted on helping Clinton with the dishes while Sheila rested. They laughed and talked among themselves with Weston chiming in occasionally until Brax dropped the diaper bag on the ground at his brother's feet.

"I'm going to help Tessa pack up the car so we can head home, so you're on diaper duty," he told Weston, handing the squirming toddler to his brother and walking backward out of the room. "Oh, and it's a smelly one!"

Kayleigh and Clinton laughed at Weston's pinched face as he stared at Walker with a mock scowl. "You just had to poop when they were busy, huh, buddy?"

Clinton leaned toward Kayleigh. "Everybody knows Brax is only out at the car *helping* so he can have an uninterrupted moment to steal kisses from his wife."

"And because he can hoist Sir Stinks-A-Lot off on me!" Weston eyeballed the ceiling and set off for a place to change his nephew.

"I'll admit, I can't imagine Weston changing a dirty diaper," she told Clinton. "Then again, I couldn't imagine him being so lively and talkative with others either, before tonight. He's always been so quiet."

Clinton wiped down the rest of the counter and rinsed out the dishrag. "Weston knows he's safe here. Knows he's loved. He's always going to be quieter than everyone else, but he's opened up so much over the years."

"I can tell he loves it here."

Clinton looked over at her. "What about your family, what are they like?"

Kayleigh handed him the last plate and pulled the plug on the dirty water, trying to give herself time to think of an answer. Eventually, she settled on the truth. "Different. It's been just my father and me for almost as long as I can remember. So, yeah, definitely different."

Just thinking of her dad made her heartsick. She prayed she'd made the right choice leaving him at the hospital. "My dad's in a coma right now. We're just waiting for him to wake up. That's why we're here. Your sons are protecting him and me."

Clinton wiped his hands off, nodding. "In that case, you're in good hands. San Antonio Security is the best in the business. Weston isn't going to let anything happen to you or your father. He's a protector through and through. Always has been."

Kayleigh nodded, knowing in her heart that Clinton was right. Weston was a natural protector and, until the merger went through, he was hers.

She just hoped it would be enough.

Chapter Fourteen

The midmorning sun was bright in Sheila and Clinton's garden where Weston knelt. Weeding was normally his favorite way to pass the time and think, but the rumble of Chance's truck pulling into their parents' driveway told him he was about to be interrupted. He met Chance halfway to the house, brushing the soil from his hands as he went.

"Where's Kayleigh?" Chance asked as the two went inside. Weston steered them to the kitchen to get Chance a cup of coffee. Between a night of peaceful sleep and the coffee he'd already had, Weston felt more energetic than since he and Kayleigh had left the lake house. But Chance had obviously been up all night on guard duty.

"She's asleep," Weston said, sliding the cup across the counter. "She's had a rough few days and I didn't feel right waking her. To be honest, I'm just glad she's sleeping at all."

Chance took a sip, nodding. "She's handling

things better than I expected. She's strong, Weston. She'll get through this."

Weston agreed wholeheartedly, but he knew firsthand how pain like losing a parent lingered. He didn't want that for Kayleigh, not anytime soon. "How are things on your end?"

"Leo's stable—no change. Luke's watching him now." Chance looked like he wanted to say more but stopped.

"What is it?"

"Something is odd at the hospital. I'm not sure exactly what it is, but it's just not normal."

Weston sat straighter. He trusted his brother's instincts. "You think Leo is in danger?"

"Not necessarily. It's just how Dr. Appleton and some of the staff is acting that's got me on edge."

Weston ran a hand over his head. This wasn't what he wanted to hear. It was bad enough suspecting people in Leo's direct employment of sharing secrets and putting the Delacruzes at risk, but if there was a nurse or doctor taking bribes, they were going to have a bigger problem.

"What have you noticed?"

Chance put his cup down. "I was there for my shift yesterday and the nurses barely checked on him. I mean, I know he's in the private section and the hospital staff have been informed of possible danger to him, but it doesn't feel right. Shouldn't they need to check his vitals more or something?"

Weston sighed and got up to pour himself another cup of coffee. Looked like he was going to need it. "Maybe there's nothing they can do but wait. They have him monitored."

Chance shrugged. "Maybe. I hope so."

"Have Maci do a background check on anyone at the hospital coming in contact with Leo. Make sure anyone guarding the door is keeping an eye out for out-of-place stuff. In the meantime, what does the doctor say about his condition?"

"No change."

"Anybody harassing the team about being there?"

"None. They've been working with us easily enough. Much better than Jasper and his misfits."

Weston took a sip of his coffee. "At least we don't have to worry about him anymore. Where are we on suspects?"

"Oliver Lyle is still the one who seems to have the most to lose and is most likely to use violent means—" He cut himself off at the squeak of someone on the stairs.

A moment later, Kayleigh appeared, dressed and ready to go for the day. She still had dark circles under her eyes, but definitely looked better than she had.

"Morning," she said, looking between the brothers as she made herself a cup of coffee. "Any news on my father?"

"He's still holding stable. No real change," Chance said. "Let me go say hello to Mom and Dad."

He obviously didn't want to continue the info about Oliver Lyle in front of Kayleigh. But that wasn't going to work. Weston had too much respect for her to treat her with kid gloves.

"Continue about Lyle first. Kayleigh is involved, no matter what, and I'm not keeping her in the dark when it comes to her own safety."

The smile she shot him was appreciative and he held out a hand to her to pull her close.

"Basically, we confirmed everything we'd heard about him before. Not only does he have a ton to lose if the merger goes through, but he's more than willing to get violent to get what he wants. We tried to put eyes on him, but no one's seen him for three weeks."

"This Lyle guy is who you think is behind it?" Kayleigh asked.

"He has the most to lose," Weston said.

Chance leaned back against the counter. "Just because he's willing to use force doesn't mean he's responsible for anything that has happened.

But something very interesting did show up when we dug a little further. Luke just contacted me with the info on my way over here, so I let him know I'd tell you."

Weston's eyes narrowed. "What's that?"

"Jasper was employed by Oliver Lyle about ten years ago."

Kayleigh's eyes got big. "Oh my gosh."

Chance nodded. "It was only for a few weeks, but there is definitely a connection there."

"Does this mean Jasper is the inside man you were talking about?" Kayleigh asked.

Weston crossed his arms at his chest. "This definitely makes it more likely. But we'll need more proof in order for anything to hold up in court."

"So, we find proof?" she asked. "How do we do that?"

"For now, we'll do some research and find out more about his connection to Lyle," Weston responded. "We can also—"

Chance's phone rang, cutting Weston off. Chance grabbed it, only to stare at the screen.

"Chance?"

"It's Maci."

"Who's Maci?"

"Our office manager," Weston told her. "Are you going to answer?"

"I'm not sure why she's video calling me.

She's supposed to be at Kayleigh's house picking up clothes."

"Maybe she has a question. Whatever it is, Maci wouldn't call you if it wasn't important. Answer it," Weston said.

Chance seemed to shake himself off and swiped for the video call. As soon as he saw her, he straightened, his eyes sharp on the screen. "Maci, what happened?"

"I went to Kayleigh's house, like you said, but it looks like someone broke in. Ransacked it."

Weston's stomach dropped and he looked over in time to see Kayleigh's face turn pale. Yet another blow.

"Where are you? Are you safe?"

"I'm still at the house."

Chance's knuckles whitened around the phone. "Get out and get someplace safe. You don't know if someone's still there or not. Go out to the car and—"

"There's nobody here. I'm safe where I am."

Chance stared at the ceiling as if it had all the answers to his frustrations. It was enough to make Weston nearly laugh, but he was just as worried.

"Maci," he cut in, "it's Weston. We know you can handle yourself, but we would all feel better if you were somewhere safe. At least until we got there."

"I'm telling you, I'm fine."

Chance's jaw ticked as he ground his teeth together and Weston knew that his patience was officially spent.

"Maci, this isn't up for discussion. Get out of the house and—" He stopped, the silence almost startling after his raised voice. "She hung up on me."

"We need to get over there," Weston said.

Chance was already heading for the door. "Are all women this stubborn? Why does she refuse to listen to a single thing I say to her? It's not as if security is my job, right? How could I possibly know what I'm talking about when it comes to keeping her safe? No, the pint-sized pixie knows everything about everything. I'm just the Neanderthal who refuses to use fire."

Kayleigh and Weston watched as he talked his way out the door.

"I'll meet you there!" Weston called. He wasn't sure if his brother had stopped talking to himself long enough to hear.

"Is he always that protective?" Kayleigh asked.

Weston laughed. "He's protective but usually pretty reasonable. Those two get on each other's last nerve."

Her eyes filled with laughter. It was a good

look on her, one he wouldn't mind seeing more often. "Really?"

"Oh yeah. It's nearly a duel at dawn every time they get into an argument. We have to have a mediator on hand when they're both in the office or things start flying."

Her smile got a little bigger. "Sounds like it's a love language."

He cracked his own smile. "You're probably right. But right now, Chance and I need to get over there. I'm sure the house is empty, but it still could be dangerous for her."

"I want to come with you."

Weston's head was shaking before his mind even comprehended the question. "I know, but you can't. We don't know if this is a trap to lure you out of hiding or an ambush. We don't even know if this is a distraction to keep us away from the hospital. I'm not going to risk you with so much uncertainty."

"So, what am I supposed to do while you check it out?"

"Stay here with Mom and Dad. I can video call you when we have a better understanding of what happened."

She was about to argue more. He leaned his forehead against hers. "It's not that I don't want you there, it's just too dangerous. We have no idea what might be waiting there. It would mean a lot if you stayed here while we are gone."

Kayleigh looked at the floor and Weston could see her hesitation. She didn't want to stay behind and she didn't feel safe on her own, but what else was there to do?

If they were trying to lure her out, he and Chance might not be enough to stop a kidnapping attempt. If it was a distraction to help an attack on the hospital, she'd be safer where they couldn't find her.

But it had to be her choice.

Finally, she let out a sigh. "Okay. I'll stay if you promise to video call as soon as you can."

Weston sighed, relief flooding his veins as he pulled her into a quick hug. "I promise. You'll even be able to tell us if something in particular is missing."

Kayleigh nodded, hugging him back.

"We won't be gone long, okay? You're safe with my parents, I promise."

He kissed her softly, wishing he could do more. Wishing he could stay with her.

And hoping that this break-in would give them some sort of clue as to what was going on.

Chapter Fifteen

Weston caught up to Chance by the time they were nearly to Kayleigh's house on the north side of San Antonio. He kept an eye on the cars around him in case they were being followed, because he knew Chance was in no frame of mind to do it.

When they pulled up to the house, Chance was out of his car and running to the front door before Weston could unbuckle his own his seat belt. Weston muttered a curse, pulling out his weapon as he got out of his car.

"Chance, wait!"

Chance—the most strategic of all the Patterson brothers—was rushing into a potentially dangerous situation without a plan. Weston knew why, but he doubted Chance recognized it.

He wasn't surprised when Chance threw the door open and started shouting before he'd even cleared the door frame.

"Maci! Maci, where are you?"

Weston shook his head. Chance's actions announced their presence to anyone still in the house and made them vulnerable, but Chance was running on autopilot. Logic held no sway in his mind.

And Weston knew if it was Kayleigh in this house, he'd be doing the same thing. So, he would back Chance up, even if he was being a dumbass.

Because that's what brothers did.

Both of them slid to a halt when their office manager poked her head out from the hallway before stepping into the living room with a duffel bag in hand. "I'm right here. I'm fine. No need to announce to the entire state of Texas that we're inside."

For a moment, Chance relaxed. They both drank in the sight of Maci, unharmed and as safe as she could be in the middle of a crime scene. Weston lowered his weapon, although he didn't holster it.

The second that Chance caught sight of the bag in Maci's hand, he went nuclear.

"What the hell is that?" His eyes darkened and he stepped as far into Maci's personal space as he could without pressing their bodies together.

Weston wasn't sure if it was restraint, the need for consent, or self-torture that forced his brother to keep that small bit of distance, but it made Weston's lips twitch with the ghost of a smile.

Chance's fingers flexed at his side, but Weston knew that even though he was upset, his brother wouldn't grab a woman in anger. None of the Patterson brothers would.

"You should have left the house the second that you noticed something was wrong. Instead, you packed a damned bag. Are you out of your mind?"

Maci glared at him, dropping the duffel to rest her hands on her hips. "Excuse me? I don't know who you think you're talking to that w—"

"No, I'm not kidding, Maci," Chance growled. "We're dealing with people who are actively trying to hurt Kayleigh and her father. They don't care about collateral damage. Who knows what would have happened if you'd caught them in the act. And instead of finding someplace safe to wait for us, like you should have, you stayed and packed a bag. Are you always this stupid and reckless or is it just today's luck?"

Weston winced as Maci's face froze into a type of cold fury he hoped to never be on the receiving end of. She breached the gap between them and, even with their height difference, anger made her a formidable opponent, especially when it felt like the air around them cooled twenty degrees in a heartbeat.

"Stupid? You think I'm stupid? I've been working for you guys for over a year now, Chance. This isn't the first time I've been in a dangerous situation. So, yes. I knew what I was dealing with and what I could have walked into, and I made the decision to do my job anyway. Isn't that what you're paying me for? To do my job?"

Maci continued to rant, but Chance wasn't responding anymore. Weston knew right away what was happening. Chance's body was there, but his mind was running through every terrible thing that Maci could have experienced if they hadn't been in time, if the thieves had still been in the house when she'd arrived.

All the Patterson brothers had their own childhood trauma—abuse, neglect, fear. The years before Sheila and Clinton had taken them in had shaped them in different ways. They each had their own way of dealing with the residual trauma when it popped up.

Luke resorted to his fists. Brax used his charm and words. Weston reverted to silence.

Weston dug deep into the strategic part of his mind and thought of all the possible...*everything*.

It was what was happening to Chance now— what happened when he was overwhelmed and didn't know what to do. Where most people could fight their way through the feelings and into consciousness, Chance just ran scenarios and shut down.

Weston grabbed Chance by the shirt collar

and got right in his face. He needed to break this cycle before Chance sank too far into it.

"Chance, you need to take Maci outside while I confirm the rest of the house is secure."

Chance stared at him with no indication he had any idea who Weston was. He didn't move or say anything. Damn it. Weston shoved him a little, trying to force a reaction.

"Chance! Get Maci outside where it's safe. Right now. Get Maci safe."

That did it. Chance blinked at him, recognition dawning in his eyes. "Weston?"

"Get Maci outside."

Chance looked around, and Weston could see him putting it all back together. His brother was a genius and it only took a split second.

"Right, outside."

"I'll secure the house."

Maci was staring at them both with huge eyes. Weston wasn't going to explain anything to her. That was up to Chance.

"Go with him," Weston said to her, praying she wouldn't argue.

She nodded, not saying a word when Chance took the duffel bag and led her toward the front door.

Alone, Weston cleared the house room by room. It wasn't ideal, but he wasn't going to ask Chance to leave Maci long enough to help. His first sweep confirmed that Maci was correct: there was nobody else in the house.

After holstering his weapon, Weston went back through the whole house again. Everywhere he turned, the house had been torn apart. Drawers left open and rifled through. Contents of cabinets spilled everywhere.

Papers and shards of broken ceramic mugs littered the floor in what he assumed was the office. Chairs had been overturned and a few of the desk drawers were in pieces on the ground.

The place was so destroyed, it was hard to tell if anything was missing. He'd have to call Kayleigh to get her input.

He walked through the house again. This time, he tried to imagine what whoever had broken in was doing and why. This obviously hadn't been a failed kidnapping attempt. If that were the case, it would've been smarter for the perps to have left no record of themselves so they could try again.

It almost seemed like they were searching for something… But then, why were the drawers only broken in the office?

Had the wannabe perps been optimistic at first, willing to leave things intact as they dug through the house, only to get discouraged when they didn't find what they'd come for? What was so important in Kayleigh's house that they'd trash the place to find it?

Weston didn't know, but he was determined to find out what the hell was going on.

"I CAN'T BELIEVE I agreed to stay behind," Kayleigh mumbled to herself.

She opened the cabinet and pulled down a mug. If she didn't get caffeine into her system soon, she'd scream. Kayleigh let the smell of coffee wash over her as she poured her cup, trying to let the familiar scent relax her as it usually did. It didn't work. She was too wound up.

Why had she agreed to stay here? It was her house that had been broken into. She should've been there. But when Weston had asked, she'd let him convince her otherwise.

It was everything she'd tried to avoid with her father.

"Weston is not Dad," she reminded herself. "He's trying to protect you, not surround you in bubble wrap." Nevertheless, the situation didn't sit well with her.

She was still mumbling to herself when Sheila walked into the kitchen. "Mind if I interrupt?"

Kayleigh's cheeks flooded with heat. "I guess we can add 'caught talking to herself' to the list of things I haven't enjoyed today. Can I get you a cup of coffee too?"

Sheila laughed, waving away the offer. "Trust me, I talk to myself all the time. Some days, I think it's the only way I'll get some quiet in my brain."

"I'm usually by myself, so I guess I don't even realize that I'm doing it anymore," Kayleigh said with a shrug.

"Do you want to talk about it?" Sheila asked, leaning on the counter across from Kayleigh. "I've been told I'm a pretty good listener. Raising four teenage boys, I had to learn how to perfect that skill."

Kayleigh had noticed that last night. Sheila had been aware of everything that was being said, even when the kitchen had been pretty chaotic.

Talking to others wasn't easy for Kayleigh. She wasn't quiet like Weston, but she was alone a lot. But she would try. "To be honest, I'm upset."

"With Weston?"

Kayleigh rocked her head back and forth. "I'm more upset with myself." She sighed, taking a fortifying sip of coffee before explaining, knowing Weston had filled Clinton and Sheila in on enough of what was happening for them to have a pretty good understanding.

"My father has always been protective— overly so. In his defense, some stuff happened when I was a kid to make him that way. And he has a lot of enemies, so he also tends to be paranoid. It's led to more than a few fights over the years."

"He loves you. It's hard for a parent to put those protective instincts away, even when the children are grown."

Sheila was obviously speaking from experience.

Kayleigh smiled at her. "I do understand that. And I love Dad. But I can't live with someone smothering me."

"And that's what you're afraid Weston is doing too."

Kayleigh let out a sigh. "When Weston asked me to stay behind when he went to see what happened at my house, I agreed because I trust him with my life."

She'd gotten a text a few minutes ago that there was no danger at the house and Weston would call in a while.

But here Kayleigh was, hiding and sipping coffee, allowing herself to be left behind.

Sheila smiled. "Weston is the most trustworthy human being I know. Although I have four others, including Clinton, who run very, very close seconds. Plus, Weston knows what he's doing."

"I know. And Weston didn't demand I stay behind. I'm frustrated because I didn't even try to convince him otherwise despite how I feel about Dad being overprotective. It's like the thought didn't cross my mind, and now all I can think about is that I should be there, not here."

Sheila was quiet for a second as she stepped around Kayleigh to fill a glass of water. Kayleigh could tell it was just a way for her to collect her thoughts, so she sipped her coffee and waited patiently.

Eventually, Sheila nodded to herself. "All of my boys are fierce protectors of the people around them. They've seen so much and been through the worst life can offer. I'm not sure how much Weston has told you."

"He told me about his father and the burns."

Sheila shook her head. "I'm glad he talked to you about it. It's not something he finds easy to share."

"He didn't give me much detail."

"No, that's his way. He doesn't want to burden anyone else. Wants to carry it all on his own wide shoulders." The older woman gave a sad shake of her head. "He wanted to do that even when those shoulders were much smaller and frailer."

Kayleigh had no doubt that was true. "I'm so thankful you and Clinton came into his life."

"You know, when he first came to live with us, Weston was so quiet, I honestly wondered if he'd ever talk to us. He was with us in the house and present at meals, but it was like he was trying to be a shadow on the wall. Day after day, I watched him look at the world like he was outside of it—part of it but still alone."

Kayleigh gripped her coffee cup, almost overwhelmed by the thought of a lonely, young Weston.

"One day, about three months after he started living with us, we all went out to eat together. It was nothing special, just a night I didn't want to cook. But while we were out, we took a picture. It was one of the first ones where Weston was smiling. As soon as I got it printed, I hung it in the hallway. Come here, I'll show it to you."

Kayleigh followed Sheila into the hallway by the front door. There were at least a dozen pictures there. Some of the full family, a few of the boys on their own. A couple of the women who had joined their tribe.

"This one." She pointed to an older picture of the family sitting in an Italian restaurant. The boys were all thirteen or fourteen. Brax was making a goofy face at Luke, with a fork of balled-up spaghetti in his hand. Chance had dropped his arm around Weston's shoulders.

And, sure enough, Weston was smiling. Nothing huge, but enough to see it.

"When the boys got home from school the afternoon I hung it, Weston was the only one who noticed the new photo. Everyone else ran upstairs in their normal way. I came and found him just staring at it. When he saw me, he dropped his book bag and walked over and hugged me."

Sheila dotted at the tears in her eyes. "First hug I'd ever gotten from him. Then he followed me into the kitchen and asked if he could help with dinner. He talked to me the entire time we chopped vegetables and stirred pots. From that night on, little by little, his trust grew for all of us. We adopted him a few months later."

Kayleigh had to wipe tears too.

Sheila smiled at her. "Weston thrives best when people see him, when he knows that he's a part of something. It's part of the reason he went into business with his brothers. He works best when he's a member of a team, even if he won't say so. That's why this family is so close. We're a team who will do anything for one another. If you want to be with him, you're going to be part of that team too."

"I want that more than anything."

"I'm glad to hear it."

"So, you're saying that I was right to stay here and not argue with Weston about going to my house."

Sheila reached out and squeezed Kayleigh's arm. "Weston's and his brothers' protective instincts are what make them so good at their job. San Antonio Security is one of the best for a reason."

"Dad knew that. That's why he brought Weston in."

"You're something special to Weston. I can tell by the way he looks at you. He doesn't want you to get hurt."

"I know." And she really did. But, also, she didn't want to have to be smothered just to make Weston happy, as much as she wanted him to be happy. "So, you think I should just stay put?"

"Hell no."

A surprised laugh escaped Kayleigh. She hadn't been expecting that.

"Look, I know Weston wants to protect you, and that's very noble of him, but that doesn't mean you need to wait at home. You have to do what's right for you because your needs matter too, Kayleigh. Even more so with your history with your father."

At Kayleigh's nod, Sheila continued. "You look like the type of person who needs a relationship to be equal to feel comfortable."

"I do."

"Good. You aren't a doormat, you're a partner. You'll need to show Weston that. You're welcome to stay here if you want, of course. But if you feel like this isn't where you should be, then…" She walked over to her purse and pulled out some keys. "I've got a car you're more than welcome to borrow."

Sheila was right about everything she'd said. Kayleigh needed to show Weston that she trusted him, but she trusted herself too. That she wanted to be part of the team.

"I will take you up on that. Thank you."

Sheila grinned. "Welcome to the family."

Chapter Sixteen

Kayleigh spent the entire drive to her house rehearsing exactly what she'd say to Weston if he complained about her showing up. She'd tell him she wasn't going to let him turn into her father, that she was going to make her own decisions about her life, that she wasn't the type to stay home and wait for news.

By the time she pulled into the driveway, she'd worked herself nearly into a frenzy.

She got out of the car and headed to the front door, only to find Weston already waiting for her. In the yard, Chance and a woman she didn't recognize—who must be the notorious Maci—were fighting, though they spoke too low for her to make out what they were saying.

Turning back to Weston, Kayleigh watched him look her over, making sure she was still in one piece. She opened her mouth to start her speech when he stepped back and opened the door for her.

It was all so anticlimactic.

"Did your mom call you? You don't seem surprised."

He shook his head. "No, but Dad mentioned you borrowed the car. We have GPS tracking on it, so I knew you were headed this way."

"Are you mad?"

He shrugged one shoulder. "I don't like that you came here unprotected but, honestly, I'm a little surprised you didn't arrive earlier."

"I don't want to be coddled. Smothered."

He cupped her arms. "I know. And I respect you too much to even try. You're strong, smart and capable."

Hearing those words from him eased the tension she'd been carrying since the moment she'd gotten into the vehicle. He *respected* her. That meant everything.

"But," he continued, "we also don't want to put you in more danger by leaving you unprotected. Until this is over, we've got to be sure we're working together as a team."

"You're right. I won't be reckless."

He smiled. "And I won't coddle."

She turned back to the door. "In your text you said there's no danger here?"

"No danger, but it's not pretty, Kayleigh. I'm sorry."

Woodenly, she stepped in and froze just inside the door. "Oh my gosh."

She'd expected to see some things on the ground and maybe some broken dishes, but it was so much worse than that. The whole house had been trashed.

She stepped farther in. There were feathers and stuffing from pillows everywhere, flour on the kitchen floor that she could see even from the front door. Picture frames had been thrown across the room and books laid open against the hardwood, their spines cracked unpleasantly, pages creased.

The whole place felt wrong, tainted. This was so much more than a mere break-in.

She felt Weston's warmth behind her before he spoke. "You can go wherever you want. We've already checked the house and no one else is here. You're safe."

Kayleigh didn't feel safe. As she walked through the rooms, with Weston at her back, she took in the ripped furniture, shredded clothing and destroyed pictures on the walls. Everything was ruined, and the more she saw, the more she hurt. Seeing the life she'd built for herself in pieces felt violating.

But the real damage came when she stepped into her studio.

Camera lenses had been shattered against

the hardwood, computers knocked over with cracked monitors. There was even a pile of hard drives on the floor—her photographs—each one damaged and twisted like someone had taken a hammer to them. Even the canvases on the wall had been ripped into pieces.

Her safe space was ruined. It was pure carnage.

Kayleigh's hand flew to her mouth and tears flooded her eyes as she took it all in. "Years of work, destroyed."

There were backups, of course. And any work she'd done for a particular client had already been delivered. Ultimately, almost all of it was replaceable.

Yet the very violation left her distraught.

She felt Weston's arms come around her and she was so thankful to have him to lean into.

"Who would do this?" she whispered, afraid if she spoke any louder, her voice would crack.

His arms tightened around her. "We think they were searching for something particular and either couldn't find it and got angry, or tried to cover the search up."

"Does this have anything to do with the merger? This doesn't seem anything like a kidnapping attempt."

He let her go but stayed close. "Kidnapping, no. But it definitely has to be related to the other things that have happened—the attempt at the lake, the mugging, the fire at Leo's. How exactly it's related, I'm not sure. They obviously weren't trying to get their hands on you while doing this."

Kayleigh nodded, feeling like a bobblehead when she couldn't get herself to stop. She needed to focus on what she could control. "Okay. Okay. I can handle this. Insurance will cover the damage, so that's good."

Inside, her feelings were roiling.

The cameras at her feet made her chest ache. She'd had most of them for a decade—had never gotten rid of a single one. To her, they signified years of hard work. She had built her career with those cameras and found the most important parts of her life with them. Every picture she'd taken had been one step further to living her dreams.

Now they were gone and, despite the fact that the pictures still existed, it hurt more than she'd ever expected to see this destruction.

"Is it a threat? Someone trying to get me to stop the merger?"

Weston ran a hand down her arm. "I know it's not what Leo wants, but things are obviously escalating. Stopping the merger would give you an out, remove you as a target."

She sighed, trying to push past the scene in front of her long enough to think it over.

The more she looked, the angrier she got. "No, I'm not going to stop the merger. In fact, I'm even more determined to make sure it goes through. I'm not going to make my decisions out of fear."

When Kayleigh glanced up, the look Weston gave her was one of quiet reverence and pride. It gave her the strength to reach for him and take what she needed. For the moment, it was a hug, but she couldn't help feel the energy between them building. Soon, she'd want more than just that simple touch.

"Come on, let's get out of here," he said, pulling from her embrace and taking her hand.

She led him toward her bedroom, looking through the remnants of her belongings scattered on the floor. Taking a settling breath, she let go of his hand and gathered a couple changes of clothes to add to what Maci had already put in the duffel.

They walked to the front hall, where they could hear Chance and Maci arguing outside. "What about the house? Do we need to wait for the police?"

He held the door and ushered her out. "Chance and our team will go through the house first, then he'll call his friends at the San Antonio PD to come in and document the scene. You'll need to go in and give your statement eventually, but not right now. I don't want to take a chance that whoever did this is waiting for you there."

Kayleigh's jaw tightened, but she gave in. She didn't like not having control of things; however, she knew it was temporary.

"We're heading out," Weston said to Chance as they walked to the car, grabbing the duffel. The two were still glaring at each other. "Call if you need anything, or if there's any changes we should know about. Maci, if you need a body disposal, call Brax."

Maci beamed at him. "I promise to leave Chance's body in the most obvious spot I can so everyone can see my handiwork."

Chance shook his head in disbelief and pulled his phone out, waving quickly to Weston and Kayleigh before walking off to make his call.

Weston chuckled and turned, placing a hand at Kayleigh's back to lead her to the car. "Follow me to Mom and Dad's. We'll make sure there's nobody tailing us. This could all be an elaborate plan to find out where you've been hiding."

She rubbed her temples. "I know it's probably the safest place we could be, but I don't really want to go back to your parents' house. It's lovely, and so are they, but if it's okay, I'm not in the mood to be around people right now."

He tilted his head to the side and studied her. "I can understand that."

"Is there somewhere else we can go?"

"Yes."

Always a man of such few words. But Kayleigh trusted him. She didn't need particulars.

They dropped by the Patterson house to grab their things and return the car. Kayleigh hugged both Sheila and Clinton, blinking back tears.

She wasn't saying goodbye forever, just a few days. When the merger was complete, she would go back and check on them. Whether Weston stayed with her or not, she wouldn't let go of Clinton and Sheila, not when they seemed to see her for exactly who she was.

As if she'd conjured him, Weston stepped into the kitchen where she was talking to the older couple. He didn't say anything, but he smiled.

Kayleigh hefted the duffel onto her shoulder, only getting as far as the doorway before Weston plucked it from her to carry himself. He kissed his parents and they made their way to the car, back seat containing all the leftovers Sheila could talk them into taking with them.

They drove, circling around town. Kayleigh knew the drill by now and wasn't paying much attention. When they pulled into a remote neighborhood on the east side of town, she straightened slightly.

The white bungalow at the end of the long

driveway was beautiful with its charcoal shutters and perfect shrubs out front.

She looked over at him. "This is your house, isn't it?"

A garage door opened in front of them and they pulled in, answering her question before he said anything.

"Yep."

Suddenly, Kayleigh was nervous. She hadn't expected him to take her to his house. She was happy to be there, but knew this wasn't something he did lightly.

He led her inside. Everything about it told her he took pride in his home, and something about that made her heart flutter. It was clean, neat, organized. Looking around, she took it all in. Everything from the furniture to the curtains were simple and solid. Straightforward.

It was all so Weston.

She followed him down the hall. He dropped her bag in a spare bedroom before they made their way back to the kitchen for some food. Thanks to what Sheila had sent, they didn't have to cook. They ate quickly, then Kayleigh called to check on Leo.

She tried not to be disappointed when Dr. Appleton told her there'd been no changes, but her heart ached. She wanted her father to be awake.

She wanted to be safe again. She wanted things to get better.

She didn't want the merger that had cost him so much to be in her hands. But for right now, she didn't have a choice.

"Why don't you take a shower?" Weston asked, loading the dishwasher after their meal.

Kayleigh jolted, realizing she'd just been staring at her phone while her head was miles away.

"It might be good for you to relax," he continued. "It's been one thing after another for you practically nonstop. You could do with a break. When you're done, I want to show you something."

"You're probably right," she said, standing up. She was nearly to the hallway when she turned to him. "What did you want to show me?"

Weston leaned against the counter and grinned. "Shower, then you'll find out."

Something about the way he looked at her, like he was excited for her reaction, made Kayleigh's heart skip a beat. She nodded, pushing a hand through her hair before she returned to the hallway and the stairs beyond.

Back in her room, she was grateful for a private bathroom so she could be alone with her thoughts. Flipping the water on to warm up, she looked at herself in the mirror. There were heavy bags under her eyes, the rest of her face pale and sallow.

As she shucked her clothes and stepped into the shower's hot water, so many things swirled inside her head that she almost felt dizzy. Her house, her father, the explosion, the kidnap attempt. It was all too much.

So she focused on the one unwavering piece. *Weston.*

If it hadn't been for him, she couldn't imagine what state she'd be in right now. He was the reason she'd been able to hold on to her sanity through all this.

Knowing he was at her side for the long haul had a gentle warmth flowing through her.

And knowing he had brought them to his house and it was only the two of them here had that warmth turning to a much higher heat.

Chapter Seventeen

The sound of the shower running was both soothing and stressful for Weston. He knew where Kayleigh was and that she was safe, but not if she was okay.

How many more hits could one person take? Every time she stared off into space with sightless eyes, he got more concerned she might not find her way back.

Who could blame her? The levels of stress continuously flowing through her body played havoc on her system. The fact that she was keeping it together at all was amazing.

He'd worked in the protection business—military, law enforcement and then San Antonio Security—long enough to recognize and handle the strain from it. His brothers had also.

But trying to find the best way to help someone who wasn't accustomed to the pressure and tension was difficult. Weston wasn't great with words and people under the best of circumstances, but he didn't want to fail Kayleigh when she needed him most.

All he could do was make sure he was here for her and take each moment as it came.

The background noise disappeared as the shower turned off. A few minutes later, he heard Kayleigh's soft footsteps on the stairs before she entered the room in obviously well-loved shorts and a T-shirt.

Weston's breath caught. Something about the casual outfit and the way the light struck her, he could almost see the young girl she'd been when they'd met. The way her eyes lit up and her mouth curled when she saw him. It made his heart catch in the best way.

But they weren't children anymore and Kayleigh had definitely grown up. Even with residual anxiety tightening her features, she was stunning.

This woman.

Seeing her in his kitchen, fresh from the shower, with no makeup, and clothes that announced she was completely comfortable with him, made Weston realize exactly how gone he was for her.

He'd rather have a stressed-out Kayleigh in pajamas with her hair a mess than another woman dressed to the nines. He craved her softness and the way she looked at life the same way he craved solitude and space: near desperately.

Kayleigh tilted her head, smiling softly. "You okay? You look a little…perplexed."

Weston cleared his throat. He hadn't meant to stare, but it was hard not to. And now wasn't the time to share what he was thinking. That needed to be after she was out of this dangerous situation.

"Yeah. Yeah, I'm fine. How about you?"

She shrugged without answering, which was answer enough. One shower wasn't going to fix everything going on in her life.

But he could help a little bit more.

"I still want to show you something. Come with me?"

He held his hand out and tried not to be nervous. If she didn't feel comfortable following him, that was okay. He'd be disappointed but he would understand.

He couldn't help his soft, relieved exhale when she took his hand. He smiled and led her to the sliding doors just off the kitchen.

Guiding her through the backyard, he enjoyed the first vestiges of sunset on the horizon. He always enjoyed seeing the sky painted in purples and pinks with the soft clouds adding dimension. Even though he'd seen the Texas sunset a million times before, it never got old.

The sunset was a beautiful reminder that no matter what, even the roughest day ended so a new one could begin. The thought had saved him more times than he could count over the years.

Sunsets and sunrises—the irrefutable proof of time's passage—had always been Weston's favorite parts of the day. Didn't hurt that they were also the most beautiful.

So to be out here in his yard, his happy place, at this time of day was a bonus.

Being here with Kayleigh at this time of day was damned near a dream come true.

His plants were all healthy and thriving as they covered the edges of the yard and the patio. He took a great amount of pride in this backyard, even though very few people saw it. It was *his*. Caring for the plants was just as important to him as them looking good.

Kayleigh had smiled at the small outdoor furniture set on the back patio where he liked to have his coffee in the morning. He wondered if she'd join him out there. What would it feel like to start and end the day with her at that little table?

He wanted nothing more than to find out.

He led her down a path that cut through the backyard furthest from the house. It was secluded and, though he knew she trusted him, too much had happened lately to let her walk into the situation blind. She was tensing, her breathing becoming slightly more labored, although she tried to hide it.

"If you're planning to kill me, this is a pretty place to do it," she said with a wobbly laugh.

"Wrong types of nutrients for these kinds of plants, so you're safe." He offered her a smile, glad when she relaxed. "Actually, I've never taken anyone out here."

She stopped, looking surprised. "What about your family? I thought you were close."

He pulled her forward, just enough to get her feet moving again. "It's not that I haven't wanted to, but they wouldn't really understand."

"And you think I will?" He could hear the hesitation in her voice.

"I know you will."

A few more steps and they rounded the higher shrubs and she could finally see it.

"Oh," Kayleigh breathed, eyes wide as she stared.

The greenhouse wasn't huge by any means, but it was quite unique. Weston had built it himself using old windows—an eco-friendly home for his plants. The back of the building was a regular room where he'd run electricity, but the main part of the greenhouse was full of greenery.

He nudged Kayleigh forward again, opening

the door for her. While she took in the rows of plants and workbenches, he watched her face. The way she smiled at the bean pods crawling up one wall; the way she laughed at the white star clematis hanging from the ceiling, the vines dipping low to nudge at their heads as they passed.

Just being inside this place was enough to take some of the weight off Weston's shoulders. It had always been like that for him, as though the greenhouse stole his stress with its very air. He loved it.

Kayleigh bent over to sniff the sweet pea. "God, this smells amazing. Did you build this?"

Weston shoved his hands in his pockets. "Yep. After I had my yard landscaped the way I wanted, I decided to build this. Traveled to estate sales all over Texas to find the windows that would work and then pieced it together."

"And the plants? Any rhyme or reason to them?"

He looked around. "No. Just whatever struck my fancy."

She smiled hugely at that.

As she looked around, he tried to see things from a newcomer's perspective. A random assortment of flowers and herbs growing in the room gave it a heady smell. The potted mint in the corner pierced the savory scent of the rosemary the next row over.

A bundle of lavender grew in a bucket in the far corner, a test to see how the plant would handle being bound in a smaller space. His mother's favorite marigolds were bright against one wall, the orange and yellow petals lightening the area.

"It's beautifully-cared-for chaos. Each flower and bud tended to. It's wild in every way, Weston."

Kayleigh's eyes flicked to his. When she looked at him that way, he felt like he could see all the way to the artist's soul that made up so much of who she was. It was the closest to magic he'd ever been.

He was a little sad when she turned away to study more of his precious plants. "I love everything about this place."

Weston chuckled, rubbing a hand over the back of his neck. "I knew you would. Let me show you the best part."

He led her through the rows to the back wall so he could open the door there. Connected to the greenhouse proper was a small room he'd built for himself. It had taken him years, only putting in a weekend of work here and there, but the space was practically an oasis to Weston.

It was a simple room, hooked up for electricity but no water, phone or internet. A haven for him on his worst days. A place that was just his. The furniture was minimal—a bed and a huge old reading chair.

Sparse and simple, just what he needed.

"This is the coziest place. I don't think I'd ever leave here!" Kayleigh said, sitting in the chair and peering through windows connected to the greenhouse they'd just been in. "It looks like a jungle in there."

Kayleigh's passion for life bled into everything she did, even mundane things like looking at plants. He wanted her close so he could revel in it and *her* for as long as she'd let him.

"This is where I come to recenter. It's my safe space, I guess. You've been through a lot lately and I thought maybe it could be the same for you."

"Weston," she choked, standing on shaky legs before she reached for him. He wrapped her up, nuzzling the top of her head when she sighed and relaxed into his embrace. "Thank you for sharing this with me."

"I've never wanted to share this place with anyone but you."

She leaned back, looking over his face like she was waiting for the punch line, but there wasn't one. Weston had never had an inkling of a desire to show anyone the greenhouse cabin before. Not even his mother. It was the only place in the world that was truly just his.

And now it was Kayleigh's too.

They stood there quietly holding each other

until Kayleigh sighed again and loosened her arms. She chuckled, disentangling herself, and he tried not to miss the feel of her against him.

Spying the leather-bound cover of a scrapbook near the bed, Weston debated on whether or not to show it to her. Finally, he decided he had to let her see.

Hopefully, she'd understand, not think it was creepy.

He sat on the bed, patting the space next to him. She joined him, eyes darting between his face and the album as he handed it to her.

"What is this?"

"Open it." He didn't want to tell her; he wanted to see her reaction.

She opened the book and promptly stopped breathing.

"Oh my gosh," she whispered, her eyes scouring the pages of the scrapbook like she'd never seen the pictures before. Ridiculous, because she was the one who'd taken them.

Since she'd gone professional with her photography, Weston had followed her career. Every project she'd been a part of, he'd printed and put in the scrapbook, along with any news articles raving about them. He had clippings of her winning awards and volunteering with young kids glued in place beside the photos she'd taken. Pictures of small villages in far-off continents and animals who'd crept up while she'd been distracted. Beautiful forests and barren deserts.

"Why?" she asked, her voice heavy with emotion.

"Because they're you. Because your love for nature shines through in every image. Plus, each picture is like seeing the world through your eyes. It was the closest thing I could find to having you in my life again."

She flipped through the book, laughing at certain pages and telling him the stories behind some of his favorite photos. Wading through thigh-high water to cross a flooded creek for a picture of a single bird. Getting snowed in to a hotel for over a week so she could take a picture of a frozen waterfall. Weston laughed as she talked about falling off low branches in trees and embarrassing herself with locals.

When the stories were done and she'd seen the whole scrapbook, she turned to him. "I've been working on a secret project for a while now that I think you'll love."

"Oh yeah?" He raised an eyebrow. "What is it?"

"Plants that survive in circumstances that they shouldn't. I've been collecting images for years."

It sounded amazing. "What made you start that?"

Kayleigh shrugged, putting the scrapbook

back on the table and shifting to face him on the bed. "It started as a side project when I was traveling. It's always so surprising to see flowers that should wither and die, but they thrive. Like finding violets in the desert, thriving in pure sunshine, or air ferns surviving in a rain forest that should make them waterlogged. They shouldn't be able to live in those conditions, but they do."

She stopped, looking up at him with swimming eyes. "It reminds me of us. We've been through so much and yet, here we are. Thriving. I always wondered what you'd think of it. I just never expected to have a chance to tell you."

At her words, Weston couldn't help himself. He palmed the back of her head and brought their lips together. The kiss was soft and sweet, a brush between two people who obviously cared for each other.

"I've missed you," he whispered when he pulled away, his thumb tracing her bottom lip. "Even when I didn't know I was missing you, I missed you."

"I missed you too," she said, tugging him back to her.

This time, there was heat behind the kiss. Weston's hands slid around her until he could pull her onto his lap. While she gripped his hair, he let his hands wander, slowly meandering up her thighs until he slipped them under her shirt, just stroking his palms along her hips and the curve of her waist. He nearly groaned at the feel of all that soft skin.

Despite everything else going on in their world, at that moment, all he could think about was Kayleigh. He wanted to see her laid out underneath him, wanted to feel every inch of her softness against the hard lines of his body. He wanted to tell her how he felt about her with every touch.

"Off," she groaned, clawing at his shirt. He slipped it off and returned the favor, exhaling sharply when they were skin to skin.

He was positive that nothing in the world would ever feel as good as having Kayleigh Delacruz in his arms.

With a hand on her back, he rolled them so Kayleigh was lying beneath him. Her hair fanned the bed, her eyes hooded and hazy with want, her lips plump and red from his kisses. When he moved his lips to her neck, she arched into him, pressing their bodies together.

"Weston, I want you."

Hearing her say it made his blood boil with need, especially when she whispered as if afraid to speak any louder.

He understood. The little greenhouse room felt like a bubble to him too. A perfect moment in time where it was just the two of them.

The world outside the bubble held violence and fear and problems. But right now, in this place, it was only the two of them. Only passion and heat and love.

With her little sigh leading him on, he worshipped Kayleigh in every way he could—the world beyond forgotten.

Chapter Eighteen

Kayleigh woke up wrapped in Weston's arms, the sky still dark outside the window. They'd moved back into the main house after their first bout of lovemaking, just before the sun fully set. She'd had a moment to take in the room before he'd stolen her attention once more.

Weston's bedroom was all earth tones and comfort. Soft sheets and plush carpet, the smell of greenery from some of the indoor plants he had stashed on every surface. It was cozy and warm, from the art on the walls down to the pictures of his family throughout the house. She was happy to see one of her own prints hanging above his dresser. Like the house, Kayleigh couldn't help but think the room suited him perfectly.

It was still the middle of the night and she was more than content to just enjoy Weston's embrace in the silence, so she tried to stay still. Somehow she still woke him up.

"Hey there." His sleep-rough voice was enough to make Kayleigh shiver. He stroked a lock of hair out of her eyes. "Everything okay?"

"Amazing." Everything about this whole night had been amazing. She ducked to rest her chin on his chest. "Have you been awake long?"

"No. I feel like I slept better than I have in years." He gave a slightly self-conscious laugh as he wrapped his arm tighter around her.

She understood. Even years after her kidnapping, sleeping was sometimes hard. She still had to have the light on and often felt anxious when she closed her eyes. But not right now, not with Weston.

"Me too. I like waking up to you, even if it's the middle of the night," she admitted, trying not to blush even though he wouldn't be able to see it in the darkness.

It was too soon for future talks, especially with so much chaos around them. But being with him made her look forward to a time when things were more settled.

Would he want that with her? Because there was no doubt that she wanted it with him.

"I like it too." He tilted her head and pressed a sweet kiss to her lips. Kayleigh opened her mouth, to ask about the future or deepen their kiss— either one was fine with her—when Weston's phone rang.

"Damn it. Middle-of-the-night calls are never good." He picked up his phone and connected the call. "Brax, what's up?"

Kayleigh adjusted so she could sit up, but Weston's arm around her waist tightened, keeping her pressed to him. She didn't hate it one bit.

She heard the murmur of Brax's voice on the other end of the line and it wasn't long before Weston swore. "Hold on. Let me put you on speakerphone."

A press of a button and Brax's voice echoed through the room. "Dad just called. Looks like somebody is watching the house. He thinks there are two cars doing surveillance, maybe three. We've got one of our best men on Leo and we're all on our way, but you're closest to them."

Weston was already out of bed and getting dressed.

Kayleigh flipped the light on and did the same.

"I don't think it's a good idea for me to bring Kayleigh over there. If it's a trap, she'll be in more dang—" He cut off as he looked over at her. "What are you doing?"

"I'm getting dressed. We're going."

"It's not a good idea."

She raised one eyebrow. "I know you're trying to protect me, but I'm not the one in danger right now. I'm not going to let someone potentially destroy your parents' house like they did my father's."

All Kayleigh could think about were the pictures on the walls, the memories of the boys coming to live with the Pattersons, of Walker and Tessa and Claire joining the family.

That picture of Weston smiling that had changed his relationship with the Pattersons forever.

Their home was built on the strength of their family's love—not on things that could be replaced with insurance money. Kayleigh wasn't going to let anything happen to it if she could help it.

She thought Weston would argue, but he merely nodded. "Thank you."

"No need to thank me. I'm part of the team."

He looked like he wanted to say more but just nodded again.

"We're on our way," he said to Brax. "See you there."

The drive to the Pattersons' was tense and mostly silent. They didn't know what they were walking into and neither was happy about it.

Parking the car a couple of blocks away, Weston grabbed her hand and they snuck through backyards to get to Sheila and Clinton's house without announcing their presence from the front. Weston cracked open the back door and snuck Kayleigh into the house.

Sheila was standing in the hallway. "Didn't expect to see you two so soon again. Maybe next time you can both use the front door. That'll be a nice change."

Sheila's words were joking but Kayleigh could see the hint of tension that curled Sheila's shoulders. She didn't like her house being watched, understandably.

Guilt made Kayleigh's stomach clench painfully. She'd brought this trouble to their doorstep.

Like he could hear her thoughts, Weston shifted closer so his chest was warm against her back. The slight touch grounded her, brought her around to the problem at hand.

No matter how the trouble had gotten here, it was here now. They needed to help take care of it.

"Come on in," Sheila said, standing to move to the light switches. She nearly flicked one on before Weston spoke.

"Don't, Mom. I'd rather make whoever is watching think everyone in the house is sleeping."

Sheila moved her hand away, nodding to her son. "Your dad's in the living room."

Weston's hand on the small of Kayleigh's back pushed her into the next room, where Clinton was peeking out the window. When they walked in, the older man relaxed slightly.

"You're okay," Clinton said. "I was worried."

Weston stepped over to hug his father. "We were at my house when Brax called. Tell me what's going on."

Clinton looked Kayleigh over again, as if he was checking that she really was okay, and smiled at her before turning back to his son. "I was up late watching a game last night. When I went to shut the blinds, I saw the vehicles—two cars and one van. They stood out because I didn't recognize any of them. One new car on the block is nothing, but three? And a *van*? No. Something told me to keep watch, so I did. After an hour, I thought I was going nuts and was about to go to bed. Then another car pulled up and they switched drivers."

"Organized surveillance, then," Weston said, stroking Kayleigh's back absently, like he couldn't stop touching her.

Clinton agreed. "I watched them do another shift change four hours later and decided to call in the big guns. That would be you and your brothers."

Kayleigh peeked out the window blinds, careful not to make movement that would bring attention to them. The sleek black car sat in the shadows that bathed the other side of the street, but even then, she could feel whoever was inside watching. It sent goose bumps prickling down her arms.

"I don't like this," Sheila said from her position near the doorway. Kayleigh noticed with a painful lurch that she didn't come closer. She didn't feel comfortable or safe in the room now that they were being surveilled.

It hurt Kayleigh more than she'd expected to know she was the cause of it all.

"I'm so sorry," she whispered.

"For what?" Sheila asked.

Kayleigh waved her hand at the closed blinds of the window. "This. All of it. They wouldn't be here if I hadn't come. You'd still be safe. I'm so sorry I brought this to your doorstep."

Sheila clucked her tongue and moved to Kayleigh's side. With a soft smile, Sheila grabbed her hand and patted it gently. "You have nothing to feel sorry for. They'll learn—mess with one Patterson, you mess with all of us. Whoever's coming after you better watch their backs because we don't go down without a fight."

The woman smirked, hip-bumping Kayleigh to make her smile. "Besides, I'm just waiting for the day when you can visit because you want to see us, not because of anything else."

Her words shocked Kayleigh almost as much as the thread of longing that gripped her. She wanted to be part of this messy, chaotic, loving family. She wanted it more than she'd wanted anything in years.

Sheila reached over and squeezed her hand. There was more than comfort in her touch. There was heartache for her situation, determination and love. It didn't matter that they barely knew each other. Kayleigh knew she was part of Sheila's family. For the first time in twenty years, it felt like she had a mother again.

And Kayleigh would do anything to keep her. And keep her safe.

WITHIN THE NEXT thirty minutes, Weston's brothers made a stealth entrance through the back door. They'd brought equipment from the office and, within fifteen minutes of being together, were ready to make their move.

The plan was simple: a unilateral attack on all three of the surveillance cars they'd spotted. If they could take them out at once, it drastically reduced the chances of anything more dangerous happening.

With all of them in position covering the few blocks, Weston had high hopes that they'd succeed. Kayleigh would be staying in the house with Mom and Dad. The best way they could help was by keeping everything dark and quiet in the house.

"Everyone in position?" Weston's gaze darted over the street as his brothers' affirmatives came through his earpiece.

They needed to work as one unit so that none of the vehicles got word to the others. None of the Patterson men planned to use violence when taking out these watchers, but they would do whatever they had to do to protect their parents.

Weston felt the same way about protecting Kayleigh. He'd keep her safe no matter what.

They needed to find out who the surveillance team worked for. Weston's money was on Oliver Lyle. Bastard wanted to stop the merger and was gathering intel so he could make a move in the next few hours, before the merger.

Weston and his brothers weren't going to let that happen.

Weston circled the house and came up in the blind spot of the sedan, the first vehicle Dad had seen. He'd watched it through the windows while he'd spoken to his parents and there was definitely someone inside.

Brax and Chance would take the van at the end of the street. Luke had the car closest to the park. They would all move at the same time.

"Okay, let's go," Weston said. "Ready in five, four, three, two—"

On one, Weston yanked open the car door, seized the driver by the shirt and dragged him out from behind the steering wheel. He could hear the sounds of his brothers finishing their own missions, but it was all background noise because all he could see was the man in his hands.

Jasper Eeley.

Weston threw him face-first against the car, trapping him with his body before the snake could slither free. "What the hell are you doing here, Eeley? Are you attacking my parents? Working for Oliver Lyle?"

Weston jerked the bigger man's arm up his back, keeping him pinned against the sedan so he couldn't move. Jasper didn't respond.

"Report," Weston barked into his comm unit.

"Van is clear, subjects subdued," Brax said.

"Same," said Luke.

"I'm good too," Weston responded. "But you'll never guess who I found in my vehicle. Our old friend Jasper Eeley."

All three of his brothers let out curses. They echoed Weston's own sentiment.

"Patterson." Jasper finally spoke. "I know what you're thinking, but it's not right. I'm not here to hurt Kayleigh, I'm here to protect her. Don't let your brothers hurt my men for following orders."

Weston pushed him more fully into the car. "If you're so concerned about your employees' safety, you might ought to have thought of that before you came hunting my family."

"It's not like that. Just hear me out."

Weston wanted to pummel the other man. Had to use a surprising amount of restraint not to do so.

"Weston," Brax said in his ear. "Guys in the van say they're on protection duty. Surveilling for forces coming toward the house, not to see if anyone leaves."

"We can't trust them," Weston snapped.

"Agreed," Chance said. "But based on their equipment and stance when we caught them, I think they may be telling the truth. They were looking in the wrong direction."

"And three vehicles for surveillance is a little overkill," Luke chimed in.

Weston didn't want to believe any of it, but there was one last piece that struck him. *Jasper wasn't fighting.* The bigger man hadn't thrown any blows or attempted to get away. The opposite, in fact.

Sighing, Weston stepped back. "We're heading to the van. Luke, you come too."

Weston gripped Jasper's shoulder tight, wrenching his arm until the man had to walk with his back arched to avoid injury. Weston preferred not to hurt people but, in this case, had no problem with the show of violence. Not with Kayleigh's and his parents' safety at risk.

They made it to the van and Weston shoved Jasper inside to sit alongside his men. Luke took a spot by the front seats and Chance by the rear door, while Weston and Brax hovered near the side door. Every exit covered.

"It's like a clown car." Brax smirked. "You guys could start your own show."

"Why are you here?" Weston asked.

Jasper held out his hands in front of him in a show of surrender. "Like I said, we're here to help."

"Last I heard, you were fired," Chance said.

As expected, Jasper's chin lifted, his eyes narrowing. "We were put on leave, not fired. Regardless, I wasn't going to disappear when Leo needed me."

"So you decided to stake out our parents' house?" Weston asked.

"Look, your company is legit and I respect that. But that doesn't mean I was going to go sip mai tais while my employer is under attack. I have men outside the hospital watching Leo, as well as others watching Dean McClintock and Gwendolyn for their safety." Jasper stared at Weston. "And, regardless of the strain in our relationship, I wanted to do the same for Kayleigh."

Weston glanced at his brothers and they each gave him a shrug. They were all coming to the same conclusion.

It looked like Jasper was telling the truth.

Weston crossed his arms and glared down at the other man. "Tell us about Oliver Lyle. We know you were employed by him."

Jasper shifted, trying to get comfortable. Weston could tell he was holding back from grabbing the shoulder he'd wrenched.

"Yeah, nearly a decade ago, and only for two weeks. I knew right away that he wasn't the type of man I could ever work for or respect. He's a bully who thinks with his fists not his brain, so I quit. Haven't had contact with him since."

"Fine."

"What does Lyle have to do with this anyway?"

Weston shrugged. "He's a suspect. Has the most to lose from the merger going through."

Across the van, Luke cleared his throat, and everyone's eyes flipped to him. "Actually, I think we can write Lyle off as a suspect. I put Claire on it to do some electronic digging a few hours ago. She just texted me."

Luke's fiancée, Claire, was a computer genius, complete with hacking skills. So, while her results might not always be technically legal, they were generally accurate.

"Lyle signed his research company to a colleague six months ago in a silent deal, so he's got no skin in this game. Something about an ailing mother out of the country. He's been in Croatia for weeks."

Chance scrubbed a hand down his face. "That means he has no real reason to want to hurt Leo or Kayleigh."

A frown worked its way onto Weston's lips. If it wasn't Lyle, then he had no idea who was targeting Kayleigh. Who else had a vested interest in the merger? Who would gain enough money, power or influence from it to risk her life?

"Look," Jasper said, "I know you don't like me, but think about it. If I wanted to hurt your family, I would have already. We had the advantage. Your parents and Kayleigh wouldn't have stood a chance. Why would we sit in the vehicles all night?"

"I hate to admit it, but he does make a valid point," Chance said.

Yeah, Weston hated it too, but there was no proof Jasper was doing anything he shouldn't have been.

"You know what, Eeley? I'll give you the benefit of the doubt. I understand your concern, but with two days until the merger, I don't want you anywhere near Kayleigh."

Jasper opened his mouth to interrupt, but Weston held a hand out. "It'll draw too much attention if she has two separate teams working around her. Focus your energy on getting Dean to the merger."

Weston glanced over at Chance. They would also be placing their own security on Dean, in case Jasper was lying through his teeth.

"What about Leo?" Jasper asked.

"We'll keep him and Kayleigh safe. But stunts like this mean we're pulling resources that are better left elsewhere. So don't do something like this again."

"Fine," Jasper huffed.

"I'm taking Kayleigh to a safe house. I don't want to bring any possible trouble to my parents. They're not part of this," Weston said. "Take your men and get out of here. If you want to help, stay out of our way."

Jasper nodded, obviously mad, but at least smart enough not to argue. Weston was never going to be friends or even friendly colleagues with this man. They may be in the same business but they were way too different.

"Just keep her and Leo safe," Jasper said. "That's all I'm asking."

Maybe not as different as Weston thought.

"We'll have someone around the clock with Leo until he wakes up. And I'm definitely not going to let anything happen to Kayleigh."

Chapter Nineteen

It was only after Weston and his brothers made it back inside the house that Kayleigh felt like she could finally breathe again. The bat she'd been holding slumped to the floor, all her fight disappearing as the adrenaline faded.

"You okay?" Weston asked, stepping so close she had to tilt her head up to see him. His eyes ran over her face like he could see inside her mind, but Kayleigh didn't hate it. In fact, she kind of loved it.

She kind of loved *him*.

She shoved that thought away immediately, though she knew she'd take it out the next time she was alone.

"I'm fine," she said. "You guys are all okay?"

"Yes." He kissed her swiftly before stepping away. "Brax and Luke went home. Chance went back to the hospital. Ends up it wasn't as dangerous as we thought."

"Who was it out there?" Clinton asked, turning to place his gun back in the hidden safety drawer on the bottom of one of the bookshelves.

A genius place to hide a weapon, especially in a house where kids played. Kayleigh couldn't even see the drawer now that he'd shut it again.

"Jasper, Leo's head of security," Weston said.

Kayleigh couldn't stop her gasp. "He was after me? Going to hurt your parents?"

"I thought you said he was fired," Sheila said, dropping the golf club she'd picked up into the little caddy near the front door.

Weston reached out and massaged the back of Kayleigh's neck. "Technically, he was placed on leave, but either way he shouldn't have been here. He was actually trying to help. Has men watching the hospital to make sure Leo is okay, and wanted to do the same when he found out Kayleigh was here."

"Do you believe he was telling the truth?"

"Yes." Weston stared down at her, letting Kayleigh see the conviction in his eyes. "We all did. If his intention was to infiltrate this house, he could've done it before we were even aware there was a problem."

The thought made Kayleigh sick. "We have to get me out of here. I don't want to put anyone else in danger."

"I don't think anyone else will come here, but we'll put a couple of our men on the house just in case." Weston turned to his dad. "Don't go picking any fights with the friends."

Clinton chuckled. "As long as they don't start anything, I won't finish it."

Weston turned back to Kayleigh. "We've got to go. Until this merger is complete, you're going into a proper safe house."

Kayleigh nodded. She wasn't about to argue.

"Be safe," Sheila whispered as she hugged Kayleigh then turned to her son. "Take care of her."

"I will, Mom," he said, his eyes locked on Kayleigh's.

With a final hug from Clinton for both of them, they were out the door and in the car. Kayleigh stared through the window at the Pattersons' house while Weston drove them away. She hoped she'd see the adorable little house again.

Hoped her luck wouldn't run out.

They dropped by Weston's place long enough to grab their things. Kayleigh stayed in the car and dialed the hospital for an update on her dad.

When she'd called every other time, she'd talked to Dr. Appleton almost immediately, but this time she was put on hold. She waited so long she was just about to hang up and try again when someone picked up.

"Are you holding for someone?" a female voice asked.

"Yes, this is Kayleigh Delacruz. I'm calling to check on the status of my father, Leo Delacruz."

"Who?"

"Leo Delacruz. He's in a coma."

What the hell? Dad had his own dedicated staff members—a perk of the private and affluent section of the hospital he was in. Why would someone not know who he was?

"Coma? There's no one in a coma here. I'm not sure—" The woman broke off and Kayleigh could hear another voice but couldn't make out what the other person was saying. "I'm sorry. Please hold."

Kayleigh gripped the phone tighter as the elevator music played softly, trying not to panic. What did this mean? No one in a coma?

Oh God, what if Dad had died and his body had been taken to the morgue? Maybe that's why there was a new nurse who didn't know him. But surely they would've called her, right?

She threw open the car door in the garage, about to run inside to get Weston, when someone picked back up on the line.

"Hello, this is Dr. Appleton."

Thank goodness. "Dr. Appleton, this is Kayleigh. Is my father all right? The woman I talked to before didn't know who he was and I—"

"Yes, he's fine, Kayleigh. Sorry for the confusion. Um, your call got routed to the wrong department, so who you spoke to didn't have all the information."

She leaned against the car in relief. "Okay." She pressed her hand against her chest, trying to calm her thundering heart. "That scared me. My imagination went wild."

The doctor cleared his throat. "I can see how this entire situation would be stressful for you. I'm so sorry."

"No need to apologize. You're the one taking care of my father." He'd been the one there to give her updates every time she'd called.

"Right. Right."

"Has there been any change?"

She wanted Leo to wake up. Wanted him to be able to deal with this merger. She wasn't sure how important it was to him for it to go through. If he was awake, would he tell her to forget it and cancel the entire proceeding? Would he tell her it was critical the merger go through no matter what?

She wished she could talk to him for just a few minutes.

"I'm sorry. There's been no change. He's still not responsive."

"That's not normal, right?" She rubbed her eyes. "It's been two days. Shouldn't there be some sign of why he's not awake? Should we be doing something else? More?"

Dr. Appleton cleared his throat again. "Let's give it another twenty-four hours. At that point we can reevaluate."

She wasn't sure what another day would do, but didn't argue. That would get them through the merger, and once that happened, at least neither she nor Leo would be a target anymore.

"Okay. Thank you for your time."

"Sorry I don't have better news for you. We'll notify you if anything changes."

"Either way—good or bad?" she asked.

"Yes, absolutely."

Kayleigh disconnected the call, still feeling a little shaken by the whole thing but glad her father was, in fact, still alive.

She was about to go inside to help Weston when her phone buzzed in her hand. Worried it may be the hospital again, she connected the call immediately.

"Hello?"

"Kayleigh, sweetheart. How are you? Are you okay?"

"Hi, Gwendolyn." Kayleigh relaxed a little. "I'm fine. What about you?"

"I'm fine, but no one will give me any info on Leo. Said it was a security issue."

Kayleigh grimaced. "I'm sorry. They're keeping everything about Dad on lockdown. But I just talked to the doctor and nothing about Dad has changed. Stable, but still hasn't woken up."

The older woman blew out a breath. "I know this makes everything doubly difficult on you. Not only your dad in the hospital but you having to deal with this crazy merger stuff."

"Believe me, I want Dad to wake up more than anything."

"Me too, sweetheart. Me too. Is there anything I can do for you? Are you going to go ahead with everything if Leo doesn't wake up?"

Kayleigh leaned back against the hood of the car. "Honestly, I don't want to. I want to bury my head in the sand and just wait until Dad wakes up and let him take care of it. But…"

She faded off. She had to face that Leo might never wake up.

"I know, honey," Gwendolyn whispered. "It's scary. We all understand."

Between Sheila and Gwendolyn, Kayleigh felt like she'd gone from having no mother to having two.

"I am going through with the merger." She straightened. "I'm not going to let these people win, whoever they are."

"Good for you. Leo would be proud. Are you somewhere safe?"

"I'm with Weston. He's taking me to a safe house. Honestly, I don't even know where."

Gwendolyn let out a soft laugh. "That's probably best. Go somewhere no one knows and let that man keep you safe."

Kayleigh smiled as Weston entered the garage, their bags in his hands. "Here he is now, so I've got to go. But I'll be sure to keep you updated about Dad as soon as I hear something. And you've got this number if you need me."

Kayleigh hadn't had her regular phone since they'd left the hospital. Weston had said it was too easily traced. Instead she was using a disposable noncontract phone—a dumb one that couldn't be tracked.

"Thanks, hon. Take care of yourself."

"You too."

She disconnected the call and smiled at Weston. "Get everything?"

He nodded and put the bags in the back seat. "I brought all your stuff and a couple changes of clothes for me. This shouldn't be a long stay."

They got into the car. He pulled out of the garage and took them toward the south side of town. Once again, his eyes were darting around, looking for anyone who might be following.

"Anything new with Leo?" he asked as they drove.

"No change. Once the merger is over, I wanted to go there and see him myself. Talk to him.

Maybe he needs to be around people he knows—hear my voice, know everything is okay."

Weston reached over and clasped her hand. "That's a good idea. By tomorrow afternoon, the merger will be complete and there won't be any reason not to see him."

"Good. How far is the safe house?"

"Not too much farther. And calling it a safe *house* is pretty generous. It's more a fortified couple of rooms off the side of a warehouse. It's in the industrial side of town near the airport. I should warn you, there aren't even any windows."

"Oh."

"I know having to stay somewhere like that might be a little triggering for you. I'm sorry. If there was anywhere else we could go, I wouldn't bring you here."

She squeezed his hand. "I'll be okay. Thanks for the warning."

"This place has absolutely no ties to me, no associations. It's our best chance to ride out the next day and a half unscathed."

She didn't ask any more questions as they drove. She knew he was going in circles to make sure there weren't any tails. She reached into the back seat and snatched her film camera from her bag.

She hadn't touched it since the day they'd

gone out on the lake. She glanced it over. It seemed to be fine, thank goodness. "This is my last camera."

"What?"

"The mugger got my main one and the people who broke into my house destroyed the others. I'll have to replace everything. But at least I still have this one." She sighed. "As soon as I can, I'd like to get what I need to develop the pictures we took at the lake."

He nodded. She was glad he didn't suggest she take care of the hundred other things first. The photos she'd taken at the lake were special. She wanted to see them.

"What do you need for a darkroom?"

"Photo paper, changing bag, development tank and a few chemicals. It doesn't have to be overly complicated or expensive. Although so few people have film cameras anymore that darkrooms are a lost art."

"What if I had one of my brothers bring whatever you need to build a simple darkroom?"

Her eyes got big. "Really?"

He shrugged. "Doesn't sound like it would be too complicated. And if you have to be trapped in a dark, windowless room for the next day or two, you might as well make some use of that time."

The dread she'd been feeling at the thought

of the windowless building lifted a little. "That would be amazing. Of course, I can think of a few other things we can do in a darkroom."

His dimple appeared. "I'm sure we can do both."

They pulled up not long after. At first glance, the building looked like every other industrial warehouse on the block. Nothing special, which was exactly what they needed.

They gathered their things from the car and Weston unlocked the door with a pass code, not a key, and they stepped inside together.

Despite how dark it was, the building wasn't that bad. It had plenty of lamps, which they both immediately began to turn on, and some comfortable-looking furniture. Plus, it was huge. More like a studio apartment than a room in a random building.

There was a bed in the corner, a small dresser pressed to one wall near the TV, and a couch in the middle of the room. Kayleigh was pleased to find the little kitchenette stocked with some basics.

"Okay, I texted Luke and he's going to get what you need for your darkroom and bring it over in a couple hours." Weston looked around then over at her, worried. "Are you sure you'll be okay?"

"I may have some rough moments," she admitted. "But it won't be so bad. I'm thankful you're here with me."

She walked over to him and hooked her arms around his neck, pulling him down so her lips could touch the exposed skin of his throat.

"Don't you want to get situated here? Get ready to make the darkroom?" He groaned as she kissed her way toward his jaw.

"That can wait. I can think of a few other things I'd rather do right now," she whispered, her voice already husky.

Weston's fingers tangled in her hair and tilted her chin up, giving him the perfect angle to capture her lips. Kayleigh's hands slid under his shirt as he backed her into the closest wall, pressing himself tight against her so he could deepen the kiss.

They pulled apart long enough for Kayleigh to shove his shirt off and then he was back, his hands on her hips, pulling her closer as he explored her neck with lips and tongue. She was panting by the time he dropped his hands down her body to grip the back of her thighs. With a single squeeze as a warning, he lifted Kayleigh into his arms and took her to bed.

The darkroom would definitely have to wait.

Chapter Twenty

Weston woke up hours later to Kayleigh's soft breaths against his chest as she slept. He could see the gentle curves of her face in the light they had on in the bathroom. This feeling of having her wrapped around him was something he could get used to.

He glanced over at his phone and saw that it was still early morning. The lack of windows in this place made it a little disorientating.

The merger was set to take place in ten hours at an office across town. They needed to keep Kayleigh alive and safe ten more hours, then the worst of the danger will have passed.

She was still going to need help picking up the pieces of her life—figuring out what was going on with Leo's health, replacing everything destroyed over the past week—but at least no one would actively be trying to kidnap her.

Weston wanted the chance to have a normal relationship with her, one where they weren't running or hiding out. He wanted to see how she took her coffee and if she liked to sleep in on the weekends. He wanted to take her to his favorite places and watch her eyes light up behind her camera.

He didn't care what they did, he just wanted to be with her.

Ten more hours and then he could be.

Luke had brought by the materials needed for the darkroom yesterday and they'd set it up in the corner. But by the time Luke had left, Weston and Kayleigh had gotten caught back up in being with each other, and actually developing the photographs had been forgotten. But it would help pass the time today before going to the merger.

His phone vibrated next to him on the bed and he carefully separated himself from Kayleigh's sleeping form to grab it.

Chance.

"Give me a second," Weston whispered into the phone. He pulled his pants on and slipped outside so he could take the call without waking Kayleigh.

Even though he wasn't far, he locked the door behind him just in case. Kayleigh could still get out if she needed, but no one else could get in.

"I'm here. Is everything okay? Leo?" The hospital would call if there had been a change but probably not as quickly as his brothers.

"He's fine, no change. But we have a situation. There was an attack on Dean McClintock about an hour ago."

"How bad?"

"Could've been much worse—they were trying to take him out. Attacked his car on his way into his office."

Weston muttered a curse. "Why was he going to his office today of all days? We agreed everyone needed to hunker down and stay safe."

"Yeah, it was a stupid move on his part. If he hadn't had extra security, he'd be dead right now."

"Anybody hurt?"

"Yes, but not on our team. Jasper was there and took a bullet. He's in critical condition. Another one of his men was killed."

Weston dragged a hand down his face. "Damn. I guess we know for sure what side Jasper is on now."

"Last word was that he'll pull through."

"Good. We need to tighten everything."

"Agreed," Chance responded. "Brax has Dean locked away. Luke basically has all of Leo's portion of the hospital on lockdown."

"Ten more hours, Chance. We need to keep everyone alive for ten more hours then this should all blow over. We can figure out who's behind it all after that."

"I don't think we're going to have to wait that long to figure out who's behind it. We caught one of the guys in the attack against Dean this morning. He's got ties to Beau Kesler."

"What?" Kesler was the man on the other side of the merger. "Let me make sure I understand. One of the guys who tried to kill Dean is connected to the son of Leo's business nemesis?"

"Yep."

Weston frowned, trying to put the puzzle pieces together and failing. "Couldn't Kesler just walk away from the merger and stop it himself?"

"Evidently it's a hostile takeover, just like what Leo did with his father. So, while it looks better for Brighton Pharmaceuticals if Kesler shows up and leads his people through the merger, it will happen with or without him."

Weston heaved a dubious sigh. "Won't Kesler be making a ton of money from this merger, even if it's a hostile takeover? Why would he want it to fall through?"

"Revenge maybe? Leo tore apart his father's company and Kesler doesn't want him doing it again. Kesler's going to make money on the merger, but it's Leo who will gain the most. Kesler doesn't want that."

Weston grunted. Revenge would make sense.

"Kesler would have firsthand knowledge of the contract too, including Leo's conditions for the merger to go through and Kayleigh's ability to stop it."

"Exactly. So we're digging into Kesler more, seeing if we can find anything concrete to back our thoughts up. For now, like you said…ten hours."

"Do we have a plan to get everyone to the office this afternoon?" Weston asked. "If I was going to make one last move against Kayleigh, it would be on the way in. And they've already proven they're willing to kill, so that takes it to the next level."

Weston needed to know the safest routes to the office, entry points, blind spots in the cameras, everything. He wasn't taking a chance on Kayleigh's safety.

"Agreed. Luke and Claire are on routes and office safety to figure out what's best. Our surest bet is probably to change the location at the last minute. We'll still have to notify Beau Kesler, but he won't have the chance to plan anything ahead of time."

"And, unfortunately, until we have proof, he'll be able to waltz right into and out of wherever we hold the merger." Weston rubbed the back of his neck. "We'll worry about proving he's a murderer, attempted murderer, attempted kidnapper and the laundry list of other criminal activity after the merger. Today, we just keep everyone alive."

"Agreed."

"I'll be waiting for an update from you guys."

"You got it."

"Hey, Chance," Weston said before they could hang up. "Thank you. You guys have gone well above and beyond for a situation where we're not even getting paid."

Chance chuckled. "Brothers, man. You know what Mom says."

"Family is forever," they both said at the same time.

KAYLEIGH WOKE UP to the sound of Weston entering the building. "Everything okay?"

"No."

She shot out of bed. "Oh my gosh. Dad?"

Weston rushed to her. "No, he's fine. I'm sorry. There's been no change."

Her heart was still crashing against her ribs. "Okay. What happened?"

"There was an attack on Dean McClintock."

"Is he okay?"

"Yes, although one of Jasper's men was killed helping save him. Jasper was shot too."

She lowered herself slowly back down on the

bed as he told her what happened. "Oh my gosh. So, Jasper really isn't behind any of this."

"No. It looks like Beau Kesler is though. One of the men who attacked Dean has ties to Kesler."

She couldn't wrap her head around what all this meant. "I just want this to be over."

"It will be in a little over nine hours." He tugged her to standing and wrapped his arms around her.

She snuggled into him for a moment. He was right. Soon this would all be over.

She pulled back and lifted her phone from the chair serving as their bedside table. "I'm going to call and check on Dad."

"Okay. And after the merger today, we can go straight back to the hos—" He broke off when her phone rang in her hand.

Her breath caught until she realized it wasn't the hospital. "It's Gwendolyn. She probably wants an update about Dad. The hospital isn't giving her any info."

Weston nodded and Kayleigh connected the call.

"Hello? Gwendolyn?"

"Kayleigh, thank God you're alive." Gwendolyn's voice was high and thready, panicked.

"What's wrong?"

Kayleigh turned to Weston, who mouthed

speakerphone. She switched it on immediately, holding the phone between them so he could hear too.

"Gwendolyn, are you okay? What's going on?" Her shoulders tensed at the soft sobs and shallow breathing coming through the line.

"Someone just rammed my car off the road. I'm not sure what to do. I tried to call Jasper but he didn't answer. And I don't know if he can be trusted anyway."

She didn't know Jasper was in the hospital.

"Are you safe right now? Is anyone after you?" They had shot at Dean. Kayleigh couldn't stand the thought of anyone shooting at Gwendolyn.

"I don't see anybody, but I can't get my car out of the ditch. I'm outside of town, so there's not very much traffic. What should I do?"

"Gwendolyn, it's Weston. Where are you exactly?"

"I'm on Jarratt Road. I got a hotel out here because I wasn't feeling safe at my house."

Kayleigh rubbed the back of her neck. They'd been so worried about her and Leo, they hadn't thought about Gwendolyn's safety.

"Is there anywhere nearby you can get to?" Weston continued. "Somewhere with people?"

"There was a gas station about half a mile back."

"Good. Go there. Start walking right now, but stay on the line."

"Okay."

Weston put the phone on mute from their side.

"Are you going to send someone to pick her up?" Kayleigh asked.

He frowned, dragging his hand across his chin. "Yes, but we're stretched thin right now. Between you, Leo and Dean, we're out of people I trust implicitly."

Kayleigh tugged on her lip, trying and failing to think of a solution while the sounds of Gwendolyn's panicked breathing rattled through the phone as the older woman walked. "She's scared because of me, Weston. Someone tried to hurt her to get to me. I can't stand that."

He cupped her cheek. "This is not your fault. The safest thing for her would be to come here with us. We're the closest ones to her. If I pick her up, I can minimize the potential risk of bringing a tail here."

"Okay, yes. Thank you." She pressed a kiss against the hand cupping her cheek.

Weston unmuted the phone. "Gwendolyn, send the address of the gas station. We're closest to you, so I'm coming to get you."

"Thank you." Kayleigh could hear the relief bleeding out of the other woman. "Thank you so much."

"Watch out for other cars. Hide if you see any. Get to the station as quickly as you can," Weston said.

Kayleigh was glad he didn't tell her what had happened to Dean. That would just make her more panicked.

"Be safe, Gwendolyn. I'll see you in just a little while," Kayleigh said, hanging up the phone. She looked up at Weston. "I guess that means no more sex in the supersecret safe house."

He laughed, tugging her closer and pressing a kiss to her lips. "I'll make it up to you after this blows over."

"Mmm, I'll hold you to that." Kayleigh's phone vibrated with a text—the address from Gwendolyn.

"You stay here and do your thing with the photos and I'll go pick her up. This is the safest place you can be." He lifted her chin, forcing her gaze to his serious eyes. "I'll lock the door behind me. Don't leave the building for anything, okay?"

"I won't." She looked up into his brown eyes. "Weston, thank you. I haven't said that enough. You're not only keeping me safe, but the people I care about the most."

He kissed her quickly once more. "Thank me when we all survive to make it to the merger."

Chapter Twenty-One

Once Weston left, Kayleigh got coffee and headed over to the makeshift darkroom in the corner. Anything was better than sitting around worrying.

Work had always been her saving grace and it would be again now. Plus, she needed to utilize the time where she could keep everything dark before Weston returned with Gwendolyn.

She put her items in place then shut down all the lights in the room, using the gleam from her phone to make her way back to the corner. She took a breath when she switched off her phone.

Blackness surrounded her.

She had to take a moment to bring her heart rate under control and focus. She wasn't trapped. She could turn the lights on at any time if she wanted. She was in control.

Plus, this was something she loved to do.

Total darkness was only required while opening the film cassette, loading it onto the reel and placing that into the tank. She fumbled at first with the unfamiliar setup but was happy when muscle memory kicked in. She had the cassette in the tank quickly and was able to turn on the red light so she could continue the process.

No doubt digital photography was the way of the future. Film was a dying art, but it was one Kayleigh never wanted to relinquish. She loved the manual effort, the physical care it took to make sure the photos came out right. The chemicals, the measuring, the agitating, even the darkness.

Now that she had negatives, she'd be able to use her scanner to make digital copies of the images and save them forever. Or would, once she replaced her negative scanner that had been destroyed at her house.

She'd probably make physical copies too. That was the best part about developing film, watching it go from the negative into a living memory on photo paper.

Normally, she waited until she'd printed the enlarged photos to peek at her shots, but when she saw the faintest hint of Weston's smile on the film, she grabbed a magnification loupe to look.

Though the image was small, just the sight of him was enough to make Kayleigh's heart jump. She couldn't imagine a day without him in her life, not anymore.

And, hopefully, after just a few more hours it would be normal days with him. The thought made her a little giddy.

Still smiling, she took the magnifier to the other pictures. There were more of Weston and their day on the lake. Even some of her father's outrageously large lake house they'd ridden by on the boat.

Just looking at it wrinkled her nose. Unlike the cabin where she'd been with Weston, this house was cold and impersonal. Kayleigh needed comfort and joy, warmth in a home, to relax, and the ostentatious lake house didn't have any.

Kayleigh's eye dragged over more of the photos, wanting to see less of the house and more of Weston. She was skimming through with the loupe so quickly she almost missed it. She stopped and went back to a negative of the lake house.

There were two people standing on the balcony. There shouldn't have been anyone there at all. Dad wouldn't have let anyone use the house when she and Weston were hiding out at the same lake.

She hadn't really been paying attention to what she was shooting when she'd taken the shots of the house. She'd been sad about her lack of family and had been using the camera to try to hide her emotions from Weston.

She skimmed down to a picture with a clearer angle of the people on the balcony and upped the power on the loupe so she could see details more clearly.

She nearly dropped the magnifying glass when she identified who the two people were.

Gwendolyn and Beau Kesler.

Gwendolyn had met with Beau Kesler, yet at the hospital she'd said she'd never seen Beau in her life.

Gwendolyn, who Weston was on his way to *rescue*.

Kayleigh grabbed her phone and rushed out of her makeshift darkroom. With shaking fingers, she dialed Weston's number, only for it to go to voice mail after one ring.

Just to be sure it wasn't a fluke, she tried again. Voice mail.

Okay. What should she do? She had no car. She needed to call Chance, but, damn it, didn't have his number in this new phone, and it didn't have internet access capability.

She would call information and get the number for San Antonio Security. She would—

The door opened and Weston stood there.

"Oh, thank God, you're okay," Kayleigh said, nearly sprinting to the door to hug him. "Gwendolyn is the inside man. She met with Beau Kesler. How did you—"

She froze on the spot when Gwendolyn stepped out from behind him, gun in her hand pointed directly at Weston.

"Hello, Kayleigh. Let's chat, dear."

WESTON HAD KNOWN something was off from the moment he'd picked Gwendolyn up from that gas station. He'd even figured out his raging internal alarms were because her entire situation had been a setup.

But he thought it was because someone was using Gwendolyn to find them, not that *she* was the one behind everything.

The little bit of blood on her forehead—which probably wasn't even real—had been a nice touch. He hadn't gone to see her car in the ditch, he'd just wanted to get her to safety.

He'd driven them all over town, making sure no one was following, when it ended up no one needed to follow at all. The enemy had already been in the car with him.

He'd been so intent on getting her inside the safe house and out of potential harm's way, he hadn't realized he'd made a huge mistake until he'd felt the muzzle of her gun against the back of his head as he opened the door.

He'd almost made a move right then to disarm Gwendolyn, prepared to take his chances, when Kayleigh had rushed over. He hadn't been willing to take a chance with her life. And now that he had his hands restrained behind his back, he wished he'd made his move.

Kayleigh was nothing short of devastated to find out Gwendolyn wasn't who she'd pretended to be.

"Dad trusted you. *I* trusted you. I can't believe you're doing this."

Gwendolyn's face was hard and cold as she pointed the gun at Kayleigh. "There's a lot you don't know about your father. He wanted his precious baby girl protected from the truth about him."

"What are you talking about?"

"That money you so enjoy? It comes at the cost of other people. Dearest Daddy isn't the pristine businessman you think he is."

Kayleigh shook her head. "Dad may have been ruthless in some of his business endeavors, but he never did anything to justify what you're doing now. He's in a coma because of you!"

"Yeah, why don't you tell us exactly what you think Leo did and maybe we can get to the bottom of this," Weston said from where Gwendolyn had forced him to sit at the table.

He wanted to keep her there as long as possible. His brothers were already attempting to reach him on his phone—it had been vibrating in his pocket. He'd called them on the way to get Gwendolyn. When he didn't respond now, they would eventually come check to see what was going on.

Gwendolyn looked at her own phone. "Less chatting and more traveling right now. We're not staying here. Today is going to be a busy day for Kayleigh."

She pointed the gun at Weston and tilted her head toward the door, gesturing for him to move. He stayed where he was. They stared at each other for a long minute.

"Have it your way." Gwendolyn turned the weapon on Kayleigh.

Damn it. Weston didn't think Gwendolyn would shoot Kayleigh, but he wasn't taking any chances. He stood and walked to the door. Kayleigh rushed over to him and grabbed his arm.

"It's going to be okay," he whispered as they walked together.

Kayleigh nodded, but he could see the terror in her eyes. He wished he could put his arms around her. But mostly he wished he could get her out of there.

Maybe while they were driving. Maybe he could convince Gwendolyn to release him so he could drive. Between he and Kayleigh, they would be able to overpower the lone woman.

But when they got outside, Weston saw why Gwendolyn had kept checking her phone since she'd arrived. Beau Kesler was waiting, leaning against his Range Rover.

"I have to admit, I didn't think this would work," he said to Gwendolyn. "I'm impressed."

Gwendolyn shrugged. "Your attack on Dean helped make my story more believable, even though you screwed it up."

"There will be plenty of time to kill Dean McClintock. Right now, he doesn't matter." Beau's smile was slimy as he pushed off his vehicle and walked toward them. "We have the princess. That's all we need."

Weston shifted so that he was between Kayleigh and Beau. There wasn't much he could do with his hands restrained, but Beau had already proven himself willing to kill. Weston wanted Kayleigh as far from him as possible.

"Are you sure?" Gwendolyn asked.

Beau looked over at Gwendolyn. "Have I ever steered you wrong? Haven't we walked through all of this together? You lost Sarah, and now it's time for Leo to pay."

Who the hell was Sarah?

"You are going to stop this merger," Gwendolyn told Kayleigh. "Your father is a murderer and I'm not about to let him make any more money off innocent people. You are going to stop it."

"Murderer?" Kayleigh's eyes widened. "What are you talking about? Dad is not a murderer."

"My dead daughter would say otherwise."

"What?" Weston and Kayleigh said at the same time.

Kayleigh shook her head. "You never talked about a daughter."

It hadn't shown up in any of the digging San Antonio Security had done on Gwendolyn either.

"Of course not. It would've made Leo suspicious to hear that his assistant had a teenager who died because of him. Beau was able to hide all traces of Sarah from my background so Leo wouldn't know."

Beau slipped his arm around Gwendolyn. "I just wanted to help you do what's right. Leo Delacruz destroys lives."

"How?" Kayleigh whispered.

"He bought my father's pharmaceutical company," Beau said. "But instead of selling it as a whole or keeping it running as it was, Leo dismantled it."

"Everyone who was in a clinical trial—like my Sarah—was cast aside. All trials canceled. She died." Gwendolyn stiffened. "Beau rebuilt another pharmaceutical company and now Leo is trying to do the same thing again. I'm not going to let that happen. Your father has to pay for what he's done."

Beau's smile was smug. "So you're going to cancel the merger today. Not only that, you're going to sign over the rest of Leo's holdings to us while you have unprecedented power of attorney. By the end of the day, everything that was Leo Delacruz's will belong to us."

Gwendolyn stepped away from him. "We didn't talk about that. All we talked about was stopping this merger."

"Think of Sarah. This is justice. Our plan shouldn't be just about stopping Leo from doing it to other people. This is about you getting what you deserve. Now is the perfect time. Leo's out of commission. We can get everything that's coming to us."

"I won't do it," Kayleigh said. "Gwendolyn, I am so sorry for what happened to your daughter, and I'm sorry if Dad had some hand in it, but I won't sign everything over to you and especially not to Beau."

Beau dropped all pretense of being reasonable and took a threatening step toward Kayleigh. "I think you will."

Kayleigh straightened her shoulders. "If you kill me, you get nothing."

Weston yanked on the handcuffs around his wrists again, but they didn't budge. "You're going to kill us anyway. You can't afford to let us live. We know who you are and that you're behind all of this. And if anyone at the merger suspects that Kayleigh has been hurt or coerced, it won't go through anyway."

Next to Weston, Kayleigh crossed her arms over her chest. "I won't do it."

Beau nodded. "Patterson is right. We can't allow you to live."

"Beau!" Gwendolyn gasped. "This wasn't what we agreed on. Leo was the only one who was supposed to get hurt."

Beau ignored her, walking toward Weston and Kayleigh. "It's business. My father always told me that you have to take your emotions out of everything when it comes to business. Of course, Dad died of a heart attack at fifty-five, so what did he know?"

Weston stepped forward so that he was completely between Beau and Kayleigh. "Don't touch her."

"Don't worry, Mr. Hero. It's not her I'm after."

Beau's fist slammed into his belly. Weston doubled over, trying to suck in air.

Beau yanked him up and nailed him in the face, once, then again. Weston couldn't protect himself with his hands restrained behind his back. Pain exploded as he took two more hits in the gut.

"Stop!" Kayleigh yelled. "Stop, please."

"You don't want me to punch him anymore?" Beau said.

Weston turned his head to the side and spat out blood. He wanted to let Kayleigh know he was all right, but Beau was already talking again.

"You're right. Punching is rather ineffective." Beau pulled out a knife, gripped Weston by the shirt and stabbed him in the side.

Agony blistered across Weston's torso and he fell forward as Beau shoved him to the ground. He could hear Kayleigh sobbing as she dropped to the ground next to him.

"Weston." She helped him sit back up. "Oh God, are you okay?"

He glanced down as she lifted his shirt to look at the wound. It hurt like hell, but at least it was in the fleshy part of his side—nothing critical.

Before he could assure Kayleigh he'd be all right, Beau snatched her up by her hair.

"Do you see what I've done to him in just a few minutes? Imagine what I could do with some time and a little creativity. Do you want to see your boyfriend die screaming? That's what's going to happen if you don't do exactly what we said."

Weston tried to get up again but fell back to the ground with a groan when Beau kicked him.

"And after we finish with Weston, maybe we'll start on his nice foster parents. That's a great story, isn't it? How Clinton and Sheila Patterson adopted all those boys. Would you like to see them also die screaming? I can kill every member of his family."

"Family has been what this is about all along, hasn't it?"

Everyone froze, turning toward the voice of the man who'd just stepped from around the building.

Kayleigh gasped. Weston blinked, worried he'd taken too many hits.

There stood Leo. Very much *not* in a coma.

Chapter Twenty-Two

"Dad?"

Kayleigh stared at her father—looking way too healthy and alert—as she bent back down to put pressure against Weston's knife wound.

How was it even possible that he was here? With a gun in his hand, no less.

Beau was wondering the same thing. "What the hell are you doing here, old man? I thought you were in a coma."

Leo shook his head. "No coma. I just didn't know who I could trust. I knew there was someone on my most inner team who was betraying me, but I wasn't sure if it was Dean, Jasper or Gwendolyn. So, I've been pretending to be in a coma for three days, with the hospital's help, to let this play out."

Kayleigh couldn't believe what she was hearing.

"You being here doesn't change anything, Leo." Gwendolyn turned so her gun was now pointed at him. "We're not going to let this merger go through. Not going to let you kill more innocent people."

Leo kept his gun trained on Beau. Good. Hopefully, that would stop him from stabbing Weston again.

"I'm very sorry to hear about your daughter," Leo said. "That was a tragedy."

"Don't try to say you're sorry now," Beau snapped out. "You killed her daughter. You killed my father. You're a murderer. Shoot him, Gwendolyn."

Kayleigh had no doubt if Beau had had a gun in his hand, he would've shot Leo.

"He's using you," Leo said to Gwendolyn. "He hasn't given you all of the story and he's using you to make himself rich."

"What are you talking about?" Gwendolyn asked.

"Don't listen to him!" Beau yelled.

"You know the story of George Kesler and me five years ago. How I bought his business."

Gwendolyn nodded. "He was your enemy. You dismantled the company."

Leo shook his head. "You've heard how we kicked everyone out of the boardroom and it was just George and me the day of the merger?"

"Shoot him, Gwendolyn!" Beau yelled. "He's messing with your head."

Leo continued over Beau. "I didn't have any plans to dismantle the company. It was worth more as a whole. George *asked* me to dismantle it. He found out Beau—and Beau's clinical research division—was cutting corners. Their experimental medicine program? It was all fake. They weren't treating people at all. Every patient was receiving a placebo. They were falsifying data."

"He's lying!" Beau yelled.

Leo shook his head. "George asked me for help. We were going to dismantle the company together to stop Beau. Then George had a rather unfortunate heart attack, so I dismantled the company myself."

Gwendolyn turned to look at Beau. "Is this true?"

"Of course not. He's just trying to save himself."

"He's rebuilt another pharmaceutical company and is doing the same thing," Leo continued calmly. "I am so terribly sorry about your daughter and any role I played in her death. But he's the one who's making money at the cost of sick people's lives. If she was in one of his earlier trials, she was not receiving real medicine. She was going to die even if the company had survived."

Gwendolyn was wavering; Kayleigh could see it. The other woman didn't know who to believe.

"Don't listen to him." Beau slammed his fist down on his Range Rover. "This is our chance to become richer than either of us have ever dreamed."

It was the wrong thing to say.

"This wasn't about money," Gwendolyn replied. "It was never about money. Not for me."

"I know, I know," Beau backtracked. "I mean…let's get Leo's money and really make him pay. We can still use Kayleigh to stop everything and get his assets signed over to us."

"I've already removed Kayleigh's power of attorney. She's of no use to you. And I'm afraid my holdings won't be nearly as exciting as Beau thinks they will be."

"Why is that?" Gwendolyn looked back and forth between Leo and Beau.

"I'm buying out Brighton Pharmaceuticals at a substantial loss for me," Leo said gently. "Most of my fortune will be gone by the end of today."

Everyone stared at Leo. No one had been expecting this.

"I've been trying to gather enough evidence against Beau to stop him from ever hurting anyone again. The proof is inside the company. And I'm pretty sure I can find proof that his father's heart attack was no accident."

Weston pulled away from Kayleigh, getting to his feet. She didn't know how he was even still conscious.

"Weston, sit back down," she whispered. "I—"

"You're done, Beau," Leo said. "I've already gotten part of the proof I needed under the guise of preliminary walk-throughs for the merger. All that it will take now is—"

Beau dove for Gwendolyn, knocking the older woman down and snatching her gun from her hand in a split second, turning it toward Leo.

He fired before Leo even had his own weapon raised.

Weston was the only one who'd realized what was about to happen and had already launched himself at Beau. Weston hit him. It wasn't enough force to knock him over, but it caused the shot to miss Leo. Off balance, Weston fell to the ground.

With a snarl, Beau pointed his gun down at Weston. "Fine. You can die first."

Kayleigh screamed, already running toward the two men as a shot rang out. "Weston!"

But it was Beau who fell over to the side, bleeding from a wound to his chest. Weston scooted up and kicked Beau's gun away from him.

Leo kept his gun pointed at Beau as he walked forward. Gwendolyn was crying on the ground, off to the side.

Kayleigh ran over to Weston and wrapped her arms around him, pulling him close, stroking his head. "I thought Beau had shot you."

Weston tried to smile at her but it came out as a grimace. "I couldn't let him kill your father."

Leo crouched next to them both as Beau moaned on the ground in pain. "And I couldn't let him kill who I'm pretty sure is my future son-in-law."

She could hear cars screeching up on the other side of the building and Weston's brothers yelling for him. Kayleigh reached out and grasped her dad's hand, squeezing it. She still had so many questions but right now it didn't matter.

Right now, all that mattered was that the men she loved most in the world were alive and going to be all right.

Epilogue

Six months later

"I guess it's safe to say you're not marrying me for my money."

Weston grinned as he carried another box of Kayleigh's things from the moving truck into his house.

She'd been living here since the day after Beau had almost killed them. She hadn't wanted to go back to her house since the people Beau and Gwendolyn had hired to look for her camera had destroyed so much of her living space.

That had suited Weston just fine. He wanted Kayleigh next to him every day for the rest of forever.

"I won't be surprised when your dad makes another fortune. Maybe not as big as the one he had, but he's too shrewd of a businessman to stay broke for long."

Leo hadn't been lying about the toll buying

Brighton Pharmaceuticals had taken on his finances. He may have gotten proof that Beau Kesler was a killer, but it had come at a cost.

The Delacruz fortune was no more. At least, not to the extent it had been. Nearly all of Leo's properties and assets had been sold to cover what he'd spent to take down Brighton Pharmaceuticals.

He still had a couple million dollars—which Weston could've lived on for the rest of his life—but for Leo it was quite the change.

But he seemed…happy. He and Kayleigh had lunch together three or four times a week. They talked all the time.

He'd even come over to Weston's parents' house to have dinner a few times.

Leo Delacruz may no longer be a financial giant, but he was going to be just fine.

Kayleigh, who'd never wanted much to do with her father's money, didn't care that it was mostly gone. She'd replaced her destroyed cameras with the insurance money and had spent the last few months working on her passion project.

Plants that survive in circumstances that they shouldn't. She could also add a few people to that study if she wanted to. Him. Her.

Them together. And they weren't just surviving, they were *thriving*.

Beau was in prison awaiting trial for attempted murder, assault and battery, arson, and kidnapping. And that didn't even touch the charges that would be brought against him once the FDA finished sorting through his company.

He would never walk around a free man again.

The court had been a little more lenient with Gwendolyn. Leo, Kayleigh and Weston had all testified that they did not believe Gwendolyn intended or would've gone through with murder. She'd been caught up in the lies Beau had fed her.

She'd been charged with kidnapping and would spend time behind bars, but not the rest of her life.

Kayleigh was unpacking boxes as Weston brought them in. She smiled up at him and he couldn't resist plucking her up off the ground and backing her against the wall.

"I'm glad you're moving in here with me permanently," he said against her lips.

"I love you, Patterson, and I can't wait until I'm a Patterson too."

"Just a few more months." He worked his lips down the side of her neck. He would never get tired of the breathy little moans she made.

"We have to be over at your parents' in an hour," she said. But her hands clutched him closer, definitely didn't push him away.

"Plenty of time. I want to take you back out to the greenhouse to make love."

She straightened, leaning away from him. "That reminds me. I have something to show you."

He pressed his lips against hers. "Later."

She smiled. "Come on. You'll like it. We have to go out toward the greenhouse to see it."

She grabbed his hand and led him out the door—not unlike how she used to do as kids. He grinned as he followed. He hoped she'd be leading him around like this when they were in their eighties.

When they got to the greenhouse, she turned and went around to the side, staying outside. "I didn't want to tell you until I was sure it would work, but I think it's pretty safe now."

She was leading them to the part of the property he hadn't done much with yet. There were so many plant and flora options, he wasn't sure what direction to go.

It was something they could plan together.

Near the corner of the property line, she stopped and knelt down. Weston knelt next to her, looking at the little plant peeking up through the soil.

His eyes widened. "Is that a jacaranda cutting?"

She smiled. "Yes. Isn't it beautiful?"

He looped an arm around her shoulders and pulled her against him. "We'll have our very own here, just like we did when we were kids."

"Even better? This is from the one at Dad's house. I asked the new owners if I could get a stem cutting and I nursed it in a jar, then as it got a little bigger, in a pot. I planted it out here a couple weeks' ago."

"This is part of *our* tree?" Weston could barely get the words past the emotion in his throat. "God, woman. I love you."

She beamed at him. "This tree will develop deep roots and grow huge here. And every time we look at it, we'll know that our roots are deep too. And each year we'll bring our kids out here and take a family picture."

Family.

He'd been blessed beyond measure as a teenager to have found a family with Sheila and Clinton and his brothers.

Now he was even more blessed to start a family of his own with the woman he'd loved his whole life.

He couldn't wait to get started.

* * * * *

Get 3 FREE REWARDS!

We'll send you 2 FREE Books plus a FREE Mystery Gift.

FREE
Value Over
$20

Both the **Harlequin Intrigue®** and **Harlequin® Romantic Suspense** series feature compelling novels filled with heart-racing action-packed romance that will keep you on the edge of your seat.

YES! Please send me 2 FREE novels from the Harlequin Intrigue or Harlequin Romantic Suspense series and my FREE gift (gift is worth about $10 retail). After receiving them, if I don't wish to receive any more books, I can return the shipping statement marked "cancel." If I don't cancel, I will receive 6 brand-new Harlequin Intrigue Larger-Print books every month and be billed just $6.49 each in the U.S. or $6.99 each in Canada, a savings of at least 13% off the cover price, or 4 brand-new Harlequin Romantic Suspense books every month and be billed just $5.49 each in the U.S. or $6.24 each in Canada, a savings of at least 12% off the cover price. It's quite a bargain! Shipping and handling is just 50¢ per book in the U.S. and $1.25 per book in Canada.* I understand that accepting the 2 free books and gift places me under no obligation to buy anything. I can always return a shipment and cancel at any time by calling the number below. The free books and gift are mine to keep no matter what I decide.

Choose one:
☐ **Harlequin Intrigue Larger-Print**
(199/399 BPA GRMX)

☐ **Harlequin Romantic Suspense**
(240/340 BPA GRMX)

☐ **Or Try Both!**
(199/399 & 240/340 BPA GRQD)

Name (please print)

Address _____ Apt. #

City _____ State/Province _____ Zip/Postal Code

Email: Please check this box ☐ if you would like to receive newsletters and promotional emails from Harlequin Enterprises ULC and its affiliates. You can unsubscribe anytime.

Mail to the Harlequin Reader Service:
IN U.S.A.: P.O. Box 1341, Buffalo, NY 14240-8531
IN CANADA: P.O. Box 603, Fort Erie, Ontario L2A 5X3

Want to try 2 free books from another series? Call 1-800-873-8635 or visit www.ReaderService.com.

THE NORA ROBERTS COLLECTION

40% OFF!

Get to the heart of happily-ever-after in these Nora Roberts classics! Immerse yourself in the beauty of love by picking up this incredible collection written by, legendary author, Nora Roberts!

YES! Please send me the **Nora Roberts Collection**. Each book in this collection is 40% off the retail price! There are a total of 4 shipments in this collection. The shipments are yours for the low, members-only discount price of $23.96 U.S./$31.16 CDN. each, plus $1.99 U.S./$4.99 CDN. for shipping and handling. If I do not cancel, I will continue to receive four books a month for three more months. I'll pay just $23.96 U.S./$31.16 CDN., plus $1.99 U.S./$4.99 CDN. for shipping and handling per shipment.* I can always return a shipment and cancel at any time.

☐ 274 2595   ☐ 474 2595

Name (please print)

Address   Apt. #

City   State/Province   Zip/Postal Code

Mail to the Harlequin Reader Service:
IN U.S.A.: P.O. Box 1341, Buffalo, NY 14240-8531
IN CANADA: P.O. Box 603, Fort Erie, Ontario L2A 5X3